Historically Black Love

The Golden Era

painted with words
by

Danny M. Coles

Disclaimer

Pedagogy Productions 2023

Copyright, 2023

by

Danny M. Coles

I attempted to recreate experiences, situations, and dialogues to my best capability and recollection. I changed some characters out of respect toward specific individuals regarding my truth and story.

Dedicated to

Dora Robinson,

thank you for enriching and blessing my life, I will always love, honor and respect you, thank you.

Table of Contents

Republican Newspaper Article

(Springfield, Massachusetts)

BUFFY SPENCER STAFF

Friends of 22-year-old Danny Coles say he is someone who had a dream and kept it alive until it came true. This month, Coles is entering Morgan State University in Baltimore, Md., and officials at two community centers, a high school and a community college here, are acting as if it were their child who is leaving.

They describe a young man who experimented with life on the streets until his determination and a cadre of supporters won out.

His friends think it is appropriate that Coles is leaving for college while the country is celebrating the birthday of Martin Luther King Jr. The latter believed so much in education and preached perseverance.

"You know, they say it takes a village to raise a child," said Dora Robinson, the Martin Luther King Jr. Community Center executive director. "Danny's had a lot of life challenges. But there have been a lot of caring and supportive adults."

"He has had every reason to throw up his hands and say, 'Why not just fail,' " said Dunbar Community Center Executive Director Cherilyn Satterwhite." There were lots of times when we thought we had lost him. There was something.

About him - he would always come around."

The obstacles cited by Coles and his mentors include problems in his family life, lack of solid academics and encouragement toward college, financial issues, and the temptations of a neighborhood and friends going over to the wrong side of the law.

Coles had dreamed of going to Morgan State since he went on the Black college tour sponsored by the Dunbar when he was a junior at Putnam Vocational Technical High School. At that time, he studied metal fabrication, played basketball and football, and never imagined college was in his grasp.

A week ago, he was accepted at the university and headed there to start the spring semester. Last week, he proudly flashed his Morgan State student identification card around.

His academic adviser at Springfield Technical Community College, Linda Randall, said, "He could have gone either way like so many young men. There was something in him; I don't know what it was. Everyone who comes in contact with him responds to him.

"Right from the beginning, I could see a lot of potentials. He just needed to be nurtured and supported. Danny was the kind of young person looking for guidance," she said. "He made many mistakes, but he always did learn from them."

Coles attended STCC for several semesters because he could not get into Morgan State with his grades from high school. He said he dropped out of STCC once but returned mainly because Robinson would not let him work at the King Center unless he was in school.

Last summer, when Morgan State officials said they would take him as a transfer student if he got nine more STCC credits and maintained at least a 2.0-grade point average, Coles knew he was on the home stretch. He got a 3.5-grade point average and will start as a sophomore at Morgan State.

Coles does not understate his determination, but he's the first to credit the people who would not give up on him.

Drugs and Violence Beckon

When his family moved to Orleans Street when he was 15, something terrible happened - he was put in the middle of temptations of drugs, violence, and crime.

"I dipped and dabbed. I did things I shouldn't have done. I was experimenting, I guess," he said.

But something good happened, too - he found himself within walking distance of the Dunbar Community Center.

Satterwhite suggested Coles go on the black college tour.

"She picked me out of all the teenagers even though I wasn't thinking of going to college. I was trying to get through high school," he said.

When the tour reached the Morgan State campus, he felt like it was where he belonged.

Coles said his dream dimmed when he worked at various factory construction and painting jobs after high school.

"I figure this is what life would be," he said.

But, while he was sitting in a shop on State Street watching the new building go up for the King Center, he decided he belonged there too.

He began as a summer camp counselor in 1991 and stayed, running programs for youth.

"Everything changed from there," he said. "Here, I had a purpose."

Suddenly, he had three more strong women - Robinson, administrator Brenda Frye, and summer camp program director Shirley Brookings - on his side and his case.

He said he had an outstanding fine of about $1,000 to pay from a court settlement of a malicious damage case leftover from his days in the street.

State Rep. Raymond A. Jordan, D-Springfield, helped him get a job at the West Springfield entrance to the Massachusetts Turnpike.

Coles rode his bicycle there since he couldn't afford a car and earned enough money to pay the fine. He once lived in his car for a week, and he has stayed with a friend, his grandmother, and his supportive godparents at times. His relationship with his mother has improved, but many difficult times precluded him from regularly living there since he was 15.

He has stayed with Dora and her husband, Frank Robinson, for several months.

Bragging rights

When he returned from a quick trip to Baltimore to arrange financial aid and housing, he showed the student identification card to the children, ages 5 to 15, who worked at the King Center.

"They always say, 'All you talk about is education,' " Coles said. He plans to study education and become a teacher.

Ron Johnson, now director of children and family services for the Center for Human Development, was one of the men who stood behind Coles.

Coles was the first youth Johnson met when he went to work at Dunbar in 1988.

"I was impressed by his outgoing manner and his sense of purpose. He sorts of enamored himself with me. Several times, I have confronted him about his choices. But he was always receptive," Johnson said.

Johnson said that Coles is an example of the importance of community centers in young people's lives.

While Coles sits and recites role models, Johnson points out that Coles has a new responsibility.

"He's become a role model for his peers and his kids at the Martin Luther King Center. I hope he realizes that," Johnson said.

Now that they no longer must worry about whether or not Coles will be accepted at Morgan State, Satterwhite said, his friends concern themselves with more mundane matters.

"He must get sheets and towels. He's going off to college with no money, and he didn't ask us for anything," she said.

But Dunbar has contributed, and a board of directors' member made a personal contribution this week. Robinson said that her center is also trying to help.

Satterwhite's voice fills with emotion when she talks of the Coles she met at 15.

"Like many young men at that time, he struggled daily with how to become a man. He was faced with all the things our young people are faced with - drugs, violence, being part of a gang, low expectations from the schools," she said.

Because Dunbar does not let young people play basketball unless they have a C or better grade point average, Satterwhite said, staff got to see his report cards. They realized he was a consistent A or B student and sponsored him on the black college tour.

But he had not been prepared on any level for college.

"During the last five years, he has struggled," she said. "But someone like Danny makes this job worth doing." Putnam Principal Cliff Flint, who Coles lists as another mentor, laughs affectionately when asked what kind of high school student he was.

"Very energetic, with the energy not always going in the right direction. There were no dull times when Danny was around, and he was always itching about something. But there was always something warm and friendly about him," he said.

"The staff here was always on Danny, sometimes ready to throw him out. But they knew a guy with potential could put that together with athletic ability. But if he never shoots another basket or plays another football game, that's fine," Flint said.

Flint said Coles is another example that proves that someone is not performing up to standards at a given time doesn't mean they can't do it.

"When you are filled with drive, it's not good luck but a good effort that gets you there," Flint said. "I wish him a good effort."

Preface

Historically Black Love

The Golden Age

I wrote this story to help heal some of the deep wounds from this exceptional circumstance, the residuals from that relationship that have profoundly affected me ever since. I needed some clarity and closure to understand better what I was feeling, thinking, and dealing with at that time in my life.

I'm not sure she understood how I felt about her or how that relationship affected me and my life on many levels. I hope this story helps. Besides, I think it's a beautiful, warm story, so I wanted to share it and put a little love into the universe.

I believe that everything happens for a reason and a season. Writing this story has helped me better understand that reason and season. Scribing in my journal, I began to explore that crucial singular moment in my life when it hit me: I was in love for the first time.

The first time a young man discovers true love, it is monumental. It's one of his most magnificent, significant moments and should be celebrated. It is also a considerable time. Real love should be dealt with by utilizing the utmost seriousness of the mind and heart; nothing should be taken for granted. If you do not care for, protect, and nurture your love, you might miss your blessing, the opportunity of a lifetime. Most importantly, you may never get the chance at true love ever again.

As a mature man, I understand now how precious, rare, and unique love is. It supersedes anything of value on Earth. Without it, you don't have much. Real love is the essential commodity of all, and it will sustain you with all you need and give you a sense of direction and purpose. Once you experience real love, nothing else will satisfy the soul. So, hang on to it and protect it; it is sacred and a blessing.

Redbone

A slang term used to describe a very high-yellow or lite-skinned individual of the African American.

1 A Mustard Seed of Hope

Going into my senior year of high school, my mother kicked me out of her home for the second of three times during the summer of eighty-nine. One sunny afternoon in late July, while we lived in our beat-up apartment on Orleans Street, in the middle of the "Hood" or the Old Hill section of Springfield, Massachusetts, *The Birthplace of Basketball.* Linda, my mother, came home wilding and screaming in a fury of rage, demanding that I get out of her apartment. Initially, I didn't think she was serious, but she persisted. I was confused and couldn't understand why she was full of anger toward me; I thought I was on track and doing well for myself as a responsible young teenager, but I guess I was wrong.

Considering my environment and circumstances of growing up smack dead in the epicenter of the Hood and being exposed to a harsh reality of no father in the home and an environment saturated with poverty, drugs, crime, and violence every day, I was maintaining and advancing.

I had no baby-mama drama issues or serious concerns with drugs, alcohol, or criminology. I was gainfully employed, a good student with second honors, well-mannered, and liked by many of my peers. I was bold, charismatic, and confident. My *Gram,* my father's mother, would often remind me how handsome I was. I was a standout player on the varsity squads of the football and basketball teams. I aspired to attend a prep school and then pursue a college education. I wanted to *be* somebody, and I desired a fruitful and productive life, but my mother could care less about my goals, dreams, or future. She wanted me out of her house and

HISTORICALLY BLACK LOVE
The Golden Era

life and free of all responsibilities when dealing with her youngest son of three, me.

I was demonstrating potential and promise as a bright young man. Still, she couldn't and refused to acknowledge anything good about me and all my efforts and accomplishments; they all were irrelevant or in vain. She demanded that I pack my shit and get the fuck out of her house.! She was cold and heartless. I didn't understand why she was treating me in such a cruel fashion. She had no love for me.

My mother always marginalized all my efforts; everything I did was never good enough. Any reasonable parent would be proud to have raised a son of my caliber and value me as an asset, not a liability. I was bright and diligent; I had a sense of self and purpose, the qualities you develop and nurture in a young person, but my mother was heartless and ice-cold; I had to go.

I still remember the horrible moment and sad day like it was yesterday. My friend Desi was at my crib. He and I played basketball often at the Dunbar Community Center and basketball courts throughout the city. We also attended the basketball camp, P.L.A.Y. *Participate in the Lives of America's Youth* together, the program was sponsored by Nike at Hampshire College, under coach Jackson.

. Desi somehow got hold of a VHS copy of my first varsity start as a Putnam basketball player. The contest was against the High School of Commerce. I dropped eighteen points in that game and eagerly wanted to see my breakout performance on tape. I was so excited that a video even existed. I'd invited Desi to my house to watch the game, so he was there when everything went down.

HISTORICALLY BLACK LOVE
The Golden Era

The way my mother embarrassed me in front of Desi was one of the lowest moments of my teenage years. Linda exhibited absolutely no respect for my friend and me. She was as nasty and aggressive as a female Blue Nose Pitbull in heat—screaming, hollering, and throwing haymakers at me in front of my company. I felt mortified by my mother's conduct; it was so ghetto and unbecoming of a good mother and a woman.

I didn't know what set her off, but I couldn't do anything right in my mother's eyes for most of my life, and this day was no different. She was fed up with me, and from the look on my mother's face and the way she clenched her teeth and fist, I was no longer her baby son; I was her adversary, a nigga on the streets.

It felt like my mother intentionally tried to provoke me into striking her back in front of my friend. I swiftly rose off the couch, intending to protect myself, while my mom ruthlessly punched me several times in the face with power and force. I was so angry, hurt, humiliated, and embarrassed. I smashed my fist through my bedroom door, leaving a large crack down its middle. Before things got out of hand, Desi said respectfully,

"Yo, Coles, I will check with you later," and bounced from my crib.

My mother called Springfield's Finest to have me extracted from the apartment. I realized the situation was getting real, and by the cold steel look in my mother's eyes, I could see she was not playing and was dead serious. She wanted me out! I begged, pleaded, and cried

4

with my mother. I had nowhere to go, no money in my pockets, nothing to fill my belly, and no place to lay my head.

I turned things up a notch and desperately tried explaining to my mother that I was going into my senior year and wanted to graduate and be equipped with at least a high school diploma. I was gunning for an athletic scholarship, running the football, or shooting jump shots. My mother never attended any of my games; therefore, she had no sense of how nice I was or my potential as an athlete.

What kind of mother sets their offspring up to fail so blatantly? I felt like she was trying to break my spirits by sabotaging my life. She was unsympathetic and heartless to her baby son and didn't care to hear my desperate pleas; Linda was colder than a Polar Bear's toenails and wanted me out!

After attempting to negotiate with my mother and the police officers for over an hour, they explained the law to me in layman's terms. Because I was seventeen and my name wasn't stated on the lease, I was not permitted to remain on the property if my mother didn't want me to. I'm sure the police officers felt some sympathy for me and some kind of way about my mother but couldn't do anything about the situation but enforce the law or have me arrested...

It was a pitiful sad scene; I didn't know where to go or what to do. I was distraught, confused, and traumatized when the two officers escorted me out of the apartment. All I had was the clothes on my back and Jordan's III on my feet as I walked down Orleans Street.

HISTORICALLY BLACK LOVE
The Golden Era

I ended up staying with my cousin Jeff who I called Jazzy. My mother's church was renting Jeff's father, a preacher at our church, a brand-new duplex on Union, just down the block from the historic Saint John's Church, an essential component of the Underground Railroad in the mid-eighteen-hundreds.

The fearless Tubman is responsible for assisting hundreds of enslaved Africans in escaping to freedom in the North. The fugitives hid in Saint John's basement during the day and traveled under the New England moonlight at night.

Jazzy lived down the street, next to the projects and across from DeBerry Elementary School and the place where the grand community festival, the Harambee, took place each year until the early nineties. It was a few houses down from where we resided when my father, in eighty-five, placed my two older brothers, Shawn and Troy, and me on a one-way Greyhound bus back to Springfield, Massachusetts, to live with my mother and baby sister Sonja after our parent's messy separation and divorce.

My brothers and I lived with our father for two years prior. I had no idea I was coming to live permanently with my mother. I thought we were visiting them over the Christmas vacation and then returning to the Blue Grass State when we first moved to Springfield from Fort Knox, Kentucky. My father started dating my sixth-grade special education teacher; since then, he has been utterly absent from my life. No communication at all, not on birthdays or holidays, not even to check up on us to see if we needed anything; he was gone in the breeze. They eventually got married and had a son. They have been married for over thirty years; it was a very confusing time for all my siblings and me.

HISTORICALLY BLACK LOVE
The Golden Era

Jeff's father was a serious pimp preacher and had women all over the country. Shit, he probably was crushing many of the women in my mother's church. His father was always on the go and never home, so Jazzy let me crash on their couch in their modestly furnished apartment for a good month. His father was traveling down South on some church revival, so it was all good.

Jeff wasn't my cousin; we just told everybody in the Hood we were. Jazzy was a pretty boy who resembled the R&B singer Al B. Sure. He was a year older than me and a senior at the High School of Commerce. He was in good with my family and accompanied us to my mother's birthplace, Timmonsville, South Carolina, a few months earlier for our family reunion. I thought it was cool of my mother to invite Jazzy to accompany our family down South. He didn't have any siblings, and his father was never around. Jazzy and I grew tight during our two weeks down South, chasing after those southern girls on that red clay dirt road, one-stoplight town...

I started experimenting with alcohol that summer with Jazzy; Old English and Private Stock were our drinks of choice. We'd play ball in DeBerry's basketball courts until the wee early hours, three, four, and sometimes five in the mornings.

DeBerry was equipped with lights, and at night with the latest Hip-Hop mixtape thumping in the background niggas would hang out—hustling crack, smoking weed, drinking, dice throwing, and playing basketball. Public enemies *It Takes A Nation To Hold Us Back* and L.L. Cool J's, *Mama Said Knock You Out*, produced by Malley Mal, along with the sounds of mixtapes kings of Ron G and Kid Capri, were in heavy rotation on the blacktop.

7

HISTORICALLY BLACK LOVE
The Golden Era

Every so often, the drama would pop off, a fight might break out, gunshots would bus off, or the detectives would roll up on the court while a basketball game was in progress and arrest or harass someone. I witness the DTs do some foul shit; it put me on to how dirty some police are. They don't play fair at all.

We often hit up Berlin's, a soul-food hole-in-the-wall joint next to Johnson's barber shop, just up the street on Hancock, across from St. John's Church. Their crispy, tasty chicken wings with some hot sauce, baked mac & cheese, and orange C&C sodas held me down during this transition.

The summer of eighty-nine consisted of basketball, Hip-Hop, 40z of Old Gold, hood rats, and Berlin's. I did my best to avoid any drama. I had my mind on getting out of Springfield and didn't want to get caught up in petty street politics.

With the on-slot of the crack epidemic avalanching across urban America in the late eighties and early nineties, I resisted the urge and pressures to get involved in the hustling game of selling crack. It seemed like everybody and their mamas were pumping drugs back then. I knew hustling crack would be my last option if my back was up against the wall or I had run out of options or opportunities. I was content with what I had, though. Plus, my biological father instilled another of his many philosophies or words of wisdom in me.

Since I was a young kid, my father constantly reiterated to me, "Son, listen, everything that glitters are not gold! Just because something or someone is bright, shiny, and attractive, it's not always good or good for you! It could look healthy and fresh outside like a shiny red apple until you bite it and discover it's rotten and has a worm in it!"

He made sure I understood that principle and what it meant. He drilled the philosophy into my head and broke it down for me.

"Just because something looks good doesn't mean it's good for you, even a pretty girl. Some of the finest females do some of the wickedest of things." You can't trust a big but and a smile.

Most niggas I knew around that time were taking penitentiary chances to scoop up the cutie pies or the fly girls and then suffered considerable damage from the consequences of the game. I had a little gift of gab, was handsome, and held down a part-time job, so I wasn't pressed to pursue those wants that I didn't need. I was strong-minded and didn't lust after the material items, the latest fashions, and foreign cars with chrome wheels.

But I also was tethering on the "Fuck the world, don't ask me for shit!" attitude. My mother abandoned me out into the crack-infested streets; I couldn't call my father in my times of need and had no pot to piss in or a place to lay my head. My current perspective was "*Me against the world!*"; I had nothing and nothing to lose.

If not for the lingering mustard seed of hope I clandestinely clanged on to, the deep desire to be a historically Black college student, specifically at Morgan State University in Baltimore, Maryland. I'm sure I would've surrendered to the heavy pressures of the streets. Considering my current homeless circumstances, I was aware of the impossible odds it would take to accomplish the goal of being a student at an H.B.C.U. How I calculated things, if I avoided getting incarcerated or impregnating a young lady, everything else was possible.

2 Grand Ma's Love

I had only one real option remaining, my Grandmother Montgomery, my mom's mom, and where I'd received her last name as my middle designation. When Reverend *"Do-Right,"* Jazzy's father, returned to Massachusetts, I had to forfeit their fake leather couch and make my way to my grandma's house. I nervously approached my grandma's residents, off Eastern Avenue, to 85 Lebanon Street in the Six Corners section of the city.

I wasn't sure what my grandmother would say or if she would let me crash at her house. When I arrived there, I carefully articulated to my grandmother my situation and how my mother called the police and had me extracted from the home. I also expressed my deep desire to graduate with a high school diploma. Grandma Montgomery said she couldn't turn me away; I was so grateful.

My grandmother had a spare room that she used as a storage room. It was cluttered to the ceiling, filled with mad boxes and things everywhere. There wasn't much extra space to maneuver around. In the room was a small fold-up cot only three feet wide with an inch-thick mattress. My grandmother brought me a small comforter and a pillow.

I took my belongings out of a hefty plastic brown garbage bag and set up camp. During my senior year in high school, my grandmother's clustered storage room was now my bedroom; it was better than Jazzy's couch or the city streets.

HISTORICALLY BLACK LOVE
The Golden Era

My grandmother was living with her commonwealth husband, Danny. They had been together for almost 20 years, although they slept in separate bedrooms. I fawned over Danny since I was five because he was cool, and we shared the same name. That admiration died soon after I'd moved in with them; Danny flipped the script on me.

He sat me down one afternoon while my grandmother was at church and chewed me a new one, laced with swearing and cures words that of a drunken sailor, telling me in the rudest way possible I wasn't welcomed there. He said that I was obligated to hit him off with fifty dollars every two weeks, which I thought was fair, but how he expressed his feelings made me lose complete and utter respect for him.

Danny never tried to communicate with me like a man, and he didn't take the time to pick my brain and ask me any questions to better understand me or my current situation. Danny's primary objective was to make my vacation in their home as uncomfortable as possible. My grandmother never was informed; he demanded I pay him every two weeks. After our conversation, I gave Danny plenty of space while I was a guest in his place.

My grandmother's and Danny's house felt more like home. It was clean and peaceful, without screaming, yelling, abuse, and violence. My grandmother enjoyed my company and conversations. She would often cook and sometimes leave me a plate wrapped in plastic on the counter, which I could feel and appreciate her love. We often sat at the kitchen table and just chatted.

HISTORICALLY BLACK LOVE
The Golden Era

My grandmother would share colorful and detailed stories of life growing up on a farm in South Carolina. She would describe the long miles she and her siblings 'had to hike just to attend elementary school, be it in the pouring rain, blazing heat, or cold. At the same time, the white children enjoyed the privilege of riding the yellow bus to school.

She shared stories of her and my grandfather being young and in love. She also explained how he'd break her heart, forcing her to relocate to Massachusetts with three young children and one on the way. She also told me of my grandfather's illegal bootleg moonshine enterprise; I learned my grandfather had a bit of gangster in him.

Grandma Montgomery always mentioned they weren't the wealthiest family. Still, they always had plenty of good, satisfying Soul food to eat, and how everything they consumed was fresh and came directly from their farm and animals. My grandmother would describe working in the fields for the entire day, suffering under the steaming, unforgivable South Carolina sun. I didn't know how my folks tolerated it; they were strong people.

My grandmother's stories warmed my heart and transplanted me back in time, providing a feeling and lens of what life on the farm was like in the early twentieth century. I felt blessed to hear those historical stories of our family; they gave me a broader perspective of our ancestry, which I thought was quite interesting.

My grandmother didn't have the best things, but it was modern compared to my mom's raggedy apartments. She had a washer and dryer in the basement, and a fully functional modern bathroom, where I enjoyed taking a hot shower. Her Colonial, New England home was equipped with a dishwasher and microwave and an enclosed porch with a comfortable couch to sit on and enjoy the assortment of New England weather and seasons. The best thing about my new living situation, I could now invite girls over and wouldn't feel so embarrassed by the apparent poverty I was living in.

Danny worked at the Post Office on the graveyard shift. My grandmother was in bed by nine, so I would invite girls over to the house in the evenings and wouldn't have to make out in a car or some godforsaken place.

Living with my grandmother was much better because I was attracting a higher class of girls—mainly because my athletic profile improved. Last season, our basketball team advanced to the Western Mass Final Four, which expanded my social profile exposure and boosted my confidence and self-esteem. At my grandmother's, I could stunt harder with the girls and felt more confident about my living situation.

A few weeks after relocating to my grandmother's, I learned why my mother kicked me out into the world. She'd been approved for a tiny two-bedroom, Section 8 housing unit in the Reed Village projects. There was no room for her baby boy; by any means necessary, I had to go.

It blows my mind how my mother had no concerns or regard for my health, welfare, and future. I was only seventeen; many young Black boys across America were getting ravaged and slaughtered by the system and each other left and right back then.

HISTORICALLY BLACK LOVE
The Golden Era

My mother was oblivious, ignorant, and not concerned with those Black boy statistics; she didn't care to abandon me. She kicked me out into a world of wolves and full of madness, with absolutely nothing, no armor in the least bit. My mother treated me like a grown-ass man who could healthfully support and be responsible for myself, but I did not know. I was only a teenage boy and so unprepared to handle real-life scenarios.

The way my mother acted out in front of my sister, company, and police officers was uncalled for. You'd think I was guilty of a significant violation with her screaming, hollering, and all the drama. You'd assumed I stole her income-tax returns, cashed her unemployment checks, made off with her rent money, or even assaulted her. I was never guilty of any of those desecrations.

I'm not insinuating I was a choir boy or a saint; I did my little dirt but never had the police knocking at my mother's door. At the most, I was defending my honor in a fight or two, nothing more. I was far from the menace and problem child my mother claimed. I was self-sufficient, independent, street-smart, and a good son.

My mother has always manipulated my siblings, making them believe I was the worst child on Earth, and everything was my fault. I always got the most brutalists of ass whippings, belts, brooms, extension cords, and fists. You name it; my mother used it. Many times

Linda was brutal towards me since I was a five-year-old child. She always found excuses or creative ways to abuse, punish and torture

15

me. She always made me feel like I was the worst and didn't deserve anything good.

My birthday was just a regular day in my house. I better not ask for shit!" I have never celebrated my birthdays with siblings or friends, received a birthday cake, or got a present from Linda. My born day wasn't necessary; I was starved of love and affection.

The only present I received as a child, I might have been seven or eight, was the Shogun Warrior Godzilla action figure from my Aunt Dorth-Ann. I was so shocked and super surprised when my aunt handed me that big old box. I almost lost my mind running around the house. I had received something for my birthday. My aunt made me feel special.

My older brothers, Shawn and Troy, often wondered why she was so brutal towards me and punished me the worse, but as long as they weren't getting brutalized and bloodied up, they were straight as six o clock.

For the entire duration, I lived with my grandmother, we never butted heads or had any problems, and we never had any disagreements, arguments, or communication issues. It was a harmonious situation and exactly what I needed at the time. A few months after graduating with my high school diploma, I moved out of her home.

Linda and I both knew what was going on and why she treated me in such a brutal fashion, but that's another story. How my mother tried to abandon me was unforgivable; nothing is worse than not being wanted and loved by your mother. She left me in a world with no sense of hope or love. Thank God for my mother's, mother my Grand Ma's love.

3 Springfield College

While I was now living with my grandmother, by God's grace, I got lucky and was employed just around the corner on Alden Street at Springfield College, a private institute and the birthplace of basketball.

I worked at Cheney Hall, the dining facility of S.C., as a member of the evening kitchen clean-up crew. After a long enduring day of academics or vocational training, then engaged in a competitive and exhausting football or basketball practice, I'd strolled to Springfield College and steam sprayed down Chaney's greasy kitchen floors.

My senior year of high school was exhausting with so many obligations, responsibilities, and social pressures, thanks to my man, my white-boyfriend, Scott Densmore. I am positive I wouldn't have graduated without Scott La Rock's vital assistants.

Since Van Sickle Middle School, Densmore and I were tight and shared a lot in common. His father retired from a career in the Army, and we both were Hip-Hop heads. Scott put me on to reading the Hip-Hop Bible, the Source Magazine. I consumed every edition, from cover to cover, of the cultural condensed journal since he put me down.

Every morning at seven-forty sharp, with coffee in hand, La Roc would come through and scoop me up in his royal blue Toyota Corolla. As he approached my grandmother's home, you could hear the bass from his twelve-inch sub-woofer rumbling, rattling, and beating up the streets, blocks away with the latest Hip-Hop tunes. He always respectfully turned the volume down in front of her house. After long and enduring days of classes, practices, and work, Scott eased the burden of getting up for school in the mornings.

At Springfield College, the students would gleefully enter the dining hall acting as if they didn't have a care or concern in the world each evening. I used to overhear them conversating about going to bomb wild-ass parties, basketball, football games, and even homecoming. Spring break seemed monumental as they described the event; the students would return to school with fresh, golden bronze tans accompanied by the wildest stories. I desired to experience that college life.

I envied many of those Springfield College students; they were privileged white kids and didn't seem to want or need anything while I struggled and fought for everything. It seemed like they were living the best time of their young lives. They were not yet fully grown, with adult obligations and responsibilities but semi-independent, preparing for their futures that would set them up for life.

While working at Springfield College, I made some observations that troubled my young, restless spirits. I became aware that many of the athletes, janitorial, and service workers were primarily people of color, brown and black. It was obvious that most Black students were the school's athletes amongst the congregation of white students at dinner. The whole situation reinforced the "White Supremacist" construct— people of color in the United States are here to serve and entertain white people.

HISTORICALLY BLACK LOVE
The Golden Era

I realized this was life for many colored folks working at Cheney Hall. I cringed to know they had to come in daily to clean, cook, and serve these mostly white students for minimal pay to maintain and survive. I still had hope and knew this was just a pit stop. I was in high school and just paying my dues.

Most of the white students I interacted with at S.C. rarely socialized or knew any Black folks personally. Being a student at Springfield College was their first-time meeting or being exposed to people with some pigment in their skin. From what I understood, much of their knowledge and education about Black people came straight from the television, and most of what they consumed about us wasn't the most positive.

I'm sure this apparent dynamic reinforced in the student's minds—in some unconscious or subliminal manner—that they were superior in some sense. The students had to be experiencing some of what I was feeling; it was so obvious. I hated that feeling of inferiority because, in my soul, I knew it wasn't true. There was greatness in my people and me.

While being aware of those stark racial dynamics and how they troubled my soul, I never forgot the comfort and warmth I felt a year before while a junior in high school. I must thank Ms. Satterwhite, the Dunbar Community Center's Executive Director. She had the foresight to send me on the Martin Luther King Jr. Black College Tour of '89.

Out of all the Hood teenagers that frequented the Dunbar, I was the only one privileged to be a part of the Black college tour. Even though my mother only gave me *twenty dollars* for the two weeks' excursion. It was mind-expanding and exposed me to the genuine possibility of obtaining a college education.

De La Sol's *Three Feet High and Raising* was the soundtrack of the Black college tour. The chaperones allowed us to play the album throughout the excursion while we visited the colleges and universities. Every time I hear any track off the album, it brings me back to the tour. The creative music was refreshing and positive.

On the Black College Tour, we visited Morehouse, Spellman, Morris Brown, Atlanta Clark, Winston Salem, South Carolina State, North Carolina AT &T, Saint Augustine College, Norfolk State, Hampton, Howard, and Morgan State Universities. I was in awe and greatly inspired by what I observed on those Black college campuses. The seeds were planted, and I felt and experienced reflections of myself and my culture viewed from an entirely new perspective.

I could effortlessly visualize myself amongst these Black college students with backpacks roaming across campus. I could see myself engaged, learning, and participating in intense class discussions and debates. The Black college environment felt right for me; it was the place I knew I belonged.

Hip-Hop was live and thumping on every campus we visited. I heard Boogie Down Productions, Rakim, Big Daddy Kane, and Public Enemy blasting out the dorm windows and throughout the campuses. It was comforting to hear Hip-Hop, which I was familiar with and connected to. It wasn't such a glaring contrast or an inferior complex like I was exposed to while employed at Springfield College.

For the first time in my life, what I observed and was exposed to on those Black college campuses was Black Excellence. I was able to see first-hand communities of Black people coordinated with one another from top to bottom. The gatekeepers, administration, and most decision-makers were Black, quite a contrast from what I was used to growing up in New England.

The deans, professors, police, coaches, advisors, kitchen, ground workers, and students were primarily shades of brown. A sense of pride spawned from those observations. Instead of being judged on my exterior, respect dynamics were at the forefront of most relationships. Black folks dealt with you because of your reputation and character content, which helped nurture growth and development from the inside out.

I felt at Springfield College or any other PWI or Predominately White Institution, most would always see my skin color before they saw the character of my heart. I didn't want to stand out as the token black guy, the dumb-nigger athlete, or a minority affirmative action recipient. I didn't want to be looked at as a suspect threat or feel the need to prove to others how intelligent and capable I was.

I wanted to be comfortable being in and around my blackness, happiness, and all. I desired to be in an environment where my presence was celebrated and not tolerated. I was on a mission to find myself and knew it was on a Black college campus. I wanted to be in my element where I could best thrive and be appreciated for being me without compromise. The Black college tour armed me with a tangible hope and a goal to be a student at an HBCU.

At the conclusion of my senior year, I didn't receive any athletics scholarships, although I did receive a couple of letters of interest from playing college football from small New England schools, such as Bridge Water and American International College; I was aiming for D-1 universities and colleges and competition, I desired to play in front of large crowds with folks screaming my name.

After understanding the stark reality my high school wasn't equipped to support and manage college-bound athletes, our academic and athletic programs were weak and severely underfunded compared to the other city high schools, and no athletic scholarship offers were coming in my direction, my motivation to pursue college sports quickly dissipated.

After my high school basketball team advanced to the Western Mass Final Four and played downtown in the Springfield Civic Center, losing to Cathedral, I saw no need for being in school, trying to earn good grades. I had no purpose; I was done. For the remainder of the year, I sat in the back of the class, threw on my hoodie with no intentions of learning, and often fell asleep; I didn't see the point. My grades have fallen significantly, and I barely graduated.

In the final week of high school, I made the conscious decision to start smoking marijuana. The way I calculated things, I wasn't receiving any scholarships to play any college sports, and I was graduating the next week with a high school diploma. I now considered myself a grown man and didn't have anything to lose by getting high.

Junior, Vincent, and I walked a crossed the street to Memorial Hospital, sat on the benches by the flagpole, and sparked my first joint up. After a couple of pulls on the joint, the birds flying, as well as the cars in motion up and down State Street, seemed to be traveling in slow motion. The sky transformed from sky-blue into a soft hue of pink. Everything had a majestic vibe, and I felt something I had never experienced previously. Junior's emerald-green Celtic Starter jacket glimmered under the New England afternoon sun while the honeycomb waves on his head seemed to roll like the waves on the Atlantic Ocean. Vincent's clothes seemed to be extra tacky and wrinkled more than they were normally; his whole style appeared to be super sloppy. His hair looked nappy as a Mississippi slave's.

We were high as hell from that one joint. It seemed like we had to scale Mount Everest just to return to campus for lunch. When we sat at the cafeteria tables, all we could do was laugh our heads off. When Assistant Principal, Mrs. Henry, came over to our table to investigate all the commotion, out of respect, we stopped laughing for twenty seconds or so, then busted out in uncontrollable laughter. I think Mrs. Henry suspected we were high. The cheap cheese pizza slices they served seemed like a five-course meal; we devoured them like they were the last meal on Earth.

My first time getting high was a true milestone event. From that point on, I danced with the flower continuously. I thought I was ready for the world; little did I know what the world had in store for me. The awareness I gained working at Springfield College lingered within me. I knew I didn't want to become a second-class citizen and intuitively understood Morgan State University was a major piece of the puzzle I had to put together.

4 Against All Odds

Since the eighty-nine Black college tour, I knew there was something special about Morgan State University. It felt right like my future was on that campus. That feeling lingered with me throughout my trials and tribulations; somehow, someway, I had to get to Morgan. If my mind could conceive it, and in my heart, I believed it, then I knew I could achieve it.

By the skin of my teeth, I barely made it out of Springfield alive; considering all I'd survive, I was blessed to have made it to witness my twenty-first born day in many aspects. The brutal street violence and menacing narcotics game decapitated and consumed many of my cohorts.

Fueled by the raging crack cocaine epidemic avalanching across urban America, Springfield, Massachusetts, *"the City of First,"* was one of the most violent mid-size American cities in the early '90s. I was familiar with scores of my high school peers who surrendered their lives to street violence and scores gobbled up by the penile system hustling street pharmaceuticals and being involved in other serious crimes.

Boo, my road dog and Putnam High basketball teammate, our center, who stood six'6 and led our high school basketball team to back-to-back 88-89 and 89-90 Western Mass Final Four appearances, in which we played downtown in the Springfield Civic Center. Boo was nice and hadn't even fully developed his ball skills at this point in his basketball career. He was in the *Street and Smith*

26

basketball magazine as one of the top-ranked high school prospects in the Commonwealth of Massachusetts and was being heavily recruited by top colleges and universities across the country.

Coach Butler would hand Boo a stack of college letters daily at practice from Division I programs interested in Boo playing hoops for their schools. I used to sit back and imagine if I had just one of those basketball scholarship opportunities, I would take full advantage of the situation and get the hell out of Springfield.

Esteemed programs, such as the University of Connecticut, Boston College, University of Massachusetts, Providence College, University of Rhode Island, and Norte Dame University, were just a few of the many colleges interested in Boo's basketball skills. Tragically Boo became one of the many sad urban tragedies of the nineties and threw all those great opportunities out of the window by playing for the infamous streets and losing.

Because Boo's lack of discipline, poor academics, and attitude disqualified him from any opportunities to shoot a basketball for any university, he quickly descended into a life of crime on the streets.

Trying to strong-arm rob a known drug dealer in the South-End section of the city, their plans went wrong and out of control. Boo, and his codefendant shot two individuals, fatally killing one and severely wounding a pregnant woman during the may-lay. Boo is locked up in Norfolk State Prison in Massachusetts for the remainder of his natural life.

HISTORICALLY BLACK LOVE
The Golden Era

I had been hanging with Boo and Binky heavily daily for months. In fact, in the winter of 92, Boo, a couple of females, and I ventured to New York City and watched the ball drop in the middle of Time Square. Boo, Binky, and I also went to the legendary *Def Jam Tour* and witnessed Public Enemy, Run-DMC, L.L. Cool J, and the Beasties Boys all get busy. Boo was my guy.

In bold print, above the fold, on the front page of the Union News, read "*Basketball Star Arrested for Murder*!" Under the caption was a color photo of Boo with his hands behind his back and in handcuffs, wearing a bright yellow Champion sweatshirt and sporting a high-top Gumby fade haircut. His cousin Binky was standing behind him, wearing a black Champion, and had this awful look of hopelessness, despair, and fear on his face. Chills shot down my spine when I viewed the newspaper's front page; I could easily visualize myself in the photo wearing a purple Champion sweatshirt confined with Boo and Bink.

What's even more ironic about this situation, I made a conscious effort to put some distance between Boo and me just before this tragic event occurred. The energy he was emitting became dark, sinister, and corrupt. My Spidey Senses began to tingle whenever I was in Boo's presence. I sensed serious trouble was heading in Boo's direction, and I needed to be as far away from him as possible.

Just a week before the botched robbery, on the twenty-second of October, my twenty-first born day, I decided I needed to fall back and cut ties with Boo and the crew; I celebrated my special day all by my lonely and copped a forty of Old Gold. They weren't traveling in the direction or down the road I wanted, and I couldn't follow them in the order they were going. A week later, Boo and Bink's lives changed forever on Halloween by committing the tragedy.

28

HISTORICALLY BLACK LOVE
The Golden Era

Around the same time, my other close homie JM, which I had known since elementary school and spent an extensive amount of my time around his home and family, was now heavy in the game of selling large amounts of cocaine. He quickly blew up to be one of the biggest drug dealers in the mid-sized New England city.

I dabbled a few times with JM but never fully committed to the game. I had reservations and understood death or incarceration was up the road. I used to call the crack they were selling *Evil Rocks* and often tried to caution them about the game's harsh consequences. I chilled, stayed on the sidelines, and received some fringe benefits of smoking some of the best weed and cruising around the city in the most fly whips.

I knew I wasn't equipped with an infostructure to hold me down if something went wrong while hustling in the game. I couldn't fathom my freedom being snatched from me, plus I still possessed a lingering hope I could still attend Morgan State University.

From what I understood, JM and his crew were in New York City to re-up on a few birds, bricks, or kilos of cocaine and happened to get pulled over by undercover detectives in the streets of Washington Heights. Now one of my closest friends was being detained at the infamous Rikers Island. An outrageous amount of money was set for his bail, and a trial date was scheduled a year and a half into the future.

I recalled hearing some horror stories about being held on the Rock. There were infamous tales of stabbings, murders, rapes amongst all the gangs, fighting, rioting, and corruption. I was uneasy about my friend's unfortunate circumstances and hoped he could maintain and hold his head in such a ruthless and demonic environment.

I was unable at that time to jet down to Rikers Island to visit JM; my driver's license was suspended for a traffic ticket I neglected to pay. All I could do was stay prayed up and hope my homie stayed protected and returned home as soon as possible. I also seriously contemplated how easily I could've been joyriding with JM and being in that vehicle when my homie was pulled over.

My heart and head were sickening with my current circumstances. Everything seemed dark and dismal; it felt as though my world was about to collapse in on me. I had a couple of close brushes with the law and the Grim Reaper myself; I am sure it would have caught up with me if I were not exposed to something different.

If it weren't for the grace of my boss at that time, Dora Robinson, the Executive Director of the Dr. Martin Luther King Jr. Community Center, and her husband, Frank, I'm sure I would have never made it to Morgan State.

After a short, unsuccessful stint of trying to hustle in the streets, taking some penitentiary chances with a few close calls that could've ended tragically, along with being employed at several dead-end factories and soul-crushing laboring jobs, I decided I needed something new. I desired a complete change and direction in my life.

One afternoon while eating a large pepperoni slice, sitting in Frank's Pizza Shop, while peering out of the window at the newly erected

HISTORICALLY BLACK LOVE
The Golden Era

Dr. Martin Luther King Jr. Community Center from the corner of State and Andrews Streets, I was contemplating my life and the next steps I would take. I wanted a change for the better and to be a part of something constructive, positive, and productive. I was contemplating how to resolve my dilemma. Then suddenly, I was overcome by a keen sense of intuition which instructed me to go across the street to the community center and inquire about any possible employment opportunities. I completed an employment application that afternoon; my life began to transform for the better from that point on.

At the beginning of the 92 inaugural summer camp session, Mrs. Robinson provided me with an opportunity that would forever change the direction of my life. She employed me as a Senior Camp Counselor for the newly erected community center. After a successful summer camp, recognizing some potential, she offered me a position as the Gym Coordinator for the After-School programs.

Mrs. Robinson's only prerequisite for me to qualify for the position was I enroll in the local Springfield Technical Community College just up the road on State Street. She articulated to me how imperative it was for me as a young Black man to pursue my education and have the ability to create more opportunities for myself in the future.

My dream to be a student at Morgan was now resuscitated, alive, and breathing. I somehow managed to avoid the traps and pitfalls in my path and was registered as a full-time student at the local community college. Armed with a real sense of hope and all the possibilities, I hunkered down, completely disengaged from hanging around certain people and being in the streets and the clubs every

31

weekend. I locked in on cultivating myself and my education. I spent most of my time, outside of work, by myself, in the library, studying and working on building my writing and communication skills.

To expand on my education, I also began to seriously study Kempo martial arts, in which I better grasped the understanding of discipline, *"the control of the mind and body"*, and the importance of technic and breath control. Studying the Arts expanded my palette of knowledge and a better understanding of myself. I studied at the Leo Williams' Martial Arts Institute.

Since 1987, when I was sixteen, cutting through the Green Projects of Bergin Circle, off Girard Ave., hearing for the first time the magnetic poetry of the great Blastmaster KRS-One of BDP, banging out someone's boom box, I instantly and completely fell in love with Hip-Hop music.

The lyrics of *A Words From Our Sponsor,* off Boogie Down Productions, classic debut album, *Criminal Minded,* was my first introduction to the great KRS-One; it felt like he was literally inside my head; it was almost a spiritual experience or awakening of the sort. The acoustics were crystal clear. I heard every lyric, sample, cut, and scratch in such an exact manner. I was so amazed and enamored by what my ears were experiencing that I posted up against the chain link fence and consumed the entire tape amongst all the madness and chaos of the projects transpiring in front of me. From that point on, I studied everything they dropped as if I was a student in a class; I was a BDP and KRS-One disciple. The "Teacha" made it cool to be intelligent, positive, and proud to be Black in America. They helped spark and expand the conscientiousness of a whole generation of Browns and blacks in American cities. From

HISTORICALLY BLACK LOVE
The Golden Era

that point on, I was a true Hip-Hop head and began to understand the value of knowledge.

As a student at S.T.C.C., I became even more consumed with Hip-Hop. I now considered myself a Backpacker, one who preferred conscious lyrics over street anthems and Gangsta Rap. I was a student of the culture and lifestyle. Hip-Hop, at that time, was one of the few things I could relate to. A lot of what the many emcees and poets were reciting on the mic resonated deep within me; I could keenly relate to and understand their concepts, perspectives, and philosophies. Hip-Hop also expanded my perspective of other folks' cultures from across the country and the world.

During this critical time at Springfield Technical Community College, A Tribe Called Quest's *Low-End Theory,* De La Sol's *Balloon The Mind State,* and Pete Rock and CL Smooth's *Mecca and the Soul Brother* were my syllabus and helped me navigate school. I studied every element of those albums, the lyrics, metaphors, production, and credits.

With my canary yellow Sony Walk-Man, and an East Pak backpack full of the latest Hip-Hop cassettes, every day, I would escape my reality and venture into another world of street poetry and imagination. Hip-Hop was my protection and insulation in a cold world.

I felt safe and progressive on S.T.C.C.'s campus. I didn't feel so exposed to the unforgiving elements of the Hood just outside the Civil War Armory's iron fences.

33

HISTORICALLY BLACK LOVE
The Golden Era

While enrolled at Springfield Technical Community College as a full-time student, I attempted to forgive and repair the unhealthy relationship with my mother. I even helped relocate her and my baby sister out of the projects by providing her with the first, last, and security deposit to move us into a tiny duplex on the Eastside of town. After living in the basement with my mother for several months, she and I began bumping heads. She had a problem with me doing my homework at the kitchen table, and I was forbidden to have company over.

Linda would eventually tell me she used me to move out of the projects, and now it was time for me to *Get the fuck out of her house!!"*

Linda called the police, misrepresented the situation, and had me extracted and arrested; I used my only phone call to reach out to my Boss, Mrs. Robinson, to inquire if she could assist me in my tight situation. Frank and Dora picked me up from the Pearl Street Police Station at ten-thirty in the evening.

The Robinsons and I negotiated the terms of my living in their vacant apartment above their Victorian home in the Historical McKnight District. At 165 Westminster Street, it was understood and agreed I could reside in their apartment rent-free if I stayed out of the streets and pursued my education.

Dora and Frank were both educated professionals and had the skills and abilities to direct and guide me. They provided a stable environment that allowed me to concentrate on myself and my education.

HISTORICALLY BLACK LOVE
The Golden Era

After two and a half enduring years of solitude, just getting by, and dropping out of school, through it all, I endured and earned a solid 3.5 GPA and the necessary credits to transfer from Springfield Technical Community College to Morgan State University as a sophomore. I did it; against all odds, I earned my wings and got the hell out of Springfield.

5 The Black College Experience

From the beginning of my journey, since I was blessed to be a participant on the 89 Black College tour, something significant was always pulling at my heart, instructing me to find a way to get down to Maryland. I would have sacrificed just about anything to discover what that motivation was. I never constructed or derived an academic plan or strategy for advancing as a student. I didn't even have an idea what I planned to study when I arrived at Morgan; the objective was to figure things out as I went.

During the Civil War, the United States government established the *Land Grant Act of 1863* to help establish institutions of higher learning to provide more opportunities and educate the four million newly freed African slaves. The land grants provided formerly enslaved people the chance to advance in American society post-Civil War by providing them with educational opportunities and marketable skills. There are 107 Historically Black colleges and universities in the United States.

The Black College Experience is just that, an experience. It's not designed for everyone seeking a college education. Black college life is intended for a particular breed of student. HBCUs are for individuals seeking and searching for an unapologetic proud, more significant, personal experience and a closer connection to Black culture, history, the struggle, and the Black race. An old saying goes, the blacker the college, the sweeter the knowledge.

HISTORICALLY BLACK LOVE
The Golden Era

Attending a Black college is a unique experience and will forever change and transform an individual. The academic and social environments will leave a lasting impression on your character and soul in a profound manner. These unique and special qualities connect its students directly to the historical, beautiful struggles and challenges of Africans in America as direct descendants of slaves.

HBCUs also stimulate and cultivate a heightened sense of pride, responsibility, and purpose toward the African American race. These traits cannot be fabricated or duplicated at any other institutions of higher learning.

Historically Black institutions also provide educational opportunities for many African American students who might not qualify academically or financially at predominantly White or traditional colleges and universities.

With freedom comes great responsibility; the meek need not apply. You can also easily lose your way in the pressure-packed Black college life's alluring and intoxicating atmosphere. The liberty, parting, and endless temptations are enough to make even the most strong-willed step out of their comfort zones. If not contained with a strong sense of self, clear objectives, purpose, and a heap of discipline, you will come to your collegian demise quickly.

HBCUs are not for the faint at heart. You must prioritize and put what is most important first, construct a well-organized plan, and establish short and long-term goals. Apply common sense, logic, and intelligence, construct a good support team around you, and you will find a way to sustain and succeed in the Black college environment.

Dr. Hudson, an animated grey-haired African American History professor, always passionately stressed to the class there is nothing new under the sun, young people. There is always a time and place for everything. Learn how to prioritize young people. Learn how to prioritize!"

At the beginning of the '94 Spring semester, it felt like I had been sucked through a wormhole and landed in the middle of Black college life. Everything changed in a blink of an eye. I was suddenly submerged in a completely new environment and a different world.

Without any big fan fare or anybody to see me off, I boarded an Amtrak train, with everything I owned in an Army footlocker and a backpack, headed from Springfield to New York City's Penn Station, and then hopped on a bus from The Port Authority in Midtown to B-More. I was somewhat nervous to a degree. I didn't know what to expect or what was waiting for me down in Maryland. I was more eager and excited to be escaping the small, miserable Massachusetts city and prepared to embrace a new world and the next challenge of my life.

As the Amtrak train began to reach the outskirts of Westchester County heading into the boroughs of New York City, I placed my headphones on and inserted Nas, the great Queens Bridge poet's classic debut album, *Illmatic* cassette tape into my walk-man, pressed the play button and let it ride. His lyrics, production, and overall vibe and concept of the album meshed perfectly with the griminess and hard-core essence of the big city. The combination of

HISTORICALLY BLACK LOVE
The Golden Era

his lyrical compositions and the visual stimulation I was observing from the train's windows put me in a New York state of mind and brought his art to life. Nasir Jones's pictures he painted with his words blended perfectly with the flamboyant, creative, and illuminating graffiti bomb on every wall, building, and subway train as Amtrak ventured deeper into the heart of the Big Apple. The experience was something only a true Hip-Hop head could appreciate.

After a long and enduring overnight twelve-hour ride, the Peter Pan bus arrived at the bus station downtown on Haines Street around 9 A.M. Charm City's vibe was noticeably different from New England's energy. I could smell the salty Atlantic Ocean air from the Chesapeake Bay as I exited the bus.

I immediately noticed the high density of black folks, blue-collar workers, and professionals in expensive business suits moving about on downtown B-More's streets. The population wasn't as diverse as Springfield's; I was used to being in the presence and mingling with more ethnic groups, whites: Italians, Irish, Polish, and Latinos.

B-More appeared to be a predominantly black city and had that Southern hospitality trait. For the most part, the people said, "Hi," or "Good morning," or at the least cracked a smile at you—a characteristic absent from the folks up North. I caught a taxi from the bus station to the city's Northeast section, my destination, Morgan State University.

Move-in-Day was awkward; I noticed many other students moving into their dorms, accompanied and assisted by their proud and anxious parents. They all were experiencing the rites of passage moment, something I wished I could have understood; both of my parents were not involved in any aspect of my education. I shook it off and was simply grateful to be enrolled at Morgan.

After I checked in and registered amongst the organized confusion of all the newly arrived college students, I Received my key to my assigned dorm room. I anxiously rode the elevator up to the fourth floor of the New Building, a brand new, seven-story male dormitory.

When I turned the key in the doorknob to room 411 and slowly pushed the heavy wooden door open, I was welcomed by an empty modest-sized space. It was official and certified; I was now a full-time student at Morgan State University.

After coming to terms, I was finally a student at the only college I desired to attend. I sat on the edge of one of the two twin beds and reflected on the many sacrifices, the blood, sweat, and tears it took to reach this vital stage in my short life. It was overwhelming and almost impossible considering where I began the journey, but I did it, and somehow, someway, I made it to Morgan.

My roommate hadn't arrived yet, and I was anxious and curious to introduce myself to him. There were two metal desks and two up-right closets. I began to visualize how I was going to arrange and organize the living space and what posters I was going to hang on the walls. I got up and walked around the room, and just outside the big sliding window I was peering out of, I noticed a tall television antenna that stretched taller than the dorm building, the freshly painted blue and orange tennis courts below, and the Hill Field House that loomed in the distance.

HISTORICALLY BLACK LOVE
The Golden Era

Then suddenly, everything hit me at once; I was overcome with a flood of emotions; I jumped up for joy and screamed at the top of my lungs, "Yes, I did it!" I had self-actualized. I was no longer a commuter at a community college but an actual full-time student at a historically Black university. Whoa! Who would have ever thought I would be a registered student at Morgan? I defied all odds, naysayers, and obstacles.

At that moment, I experienced this strange nostalgia when I considered my new home. My dorm room could have easily been a correctional facility or a pine box if I had made one wrong decision, move, or misstep. Without the protection of a higher power, there was no doubt I was favored in more ways than one.

On my first morning as an official student at Morgan State, I ventured across the campus on a brisk cold January morning to eagerly explore and get acclimated to my new school and world. As I was making my way toward Holmes Hall on the North end of the campus, I noticed this large, powerful, and determined bronze statue erected in front of the newly rehabilitated academic hall.

The figure was a man walking with a cane; his confidence, pride, and determination could be felt in his face and demeanor. After a closer inspection of the statue, it turned out to be the great Fredrick Douglas. I was astonished and taken aback because Douglas was one of my role models and all-time heroes.

The *Narrative of the Life of Fredrick Douglas, An American Slave,* was the first book I ever read. It inspired and greatly influenced me to learn and pursue an education. While I was a student at Springfield Technical Community College, I continuously read and studied his manuscript, extracting the essence of his words.

As an enslaved person in the mid-1800s, Douglass was determined to be a free man and creatively taught himself how to read and write; then, after several attempts escaped to Massachusetts from Maryland. He ascended to become a historical ambassador for the abolition of African slaves in America.

I studied each word he wrote in his manuscript, intrigued by his will and desire to be an educated free man. Douglass's memoir was the inspiration for my transition from the streets to a scholar. I used to proudly wear my favorite black and white Fredrick Douglas t-shirt as a backpacker or a conscious Hip-Hopper. I took the Fredrick Douglas statue as a celestial indicator. I was on the right course, where I was supposed to be at Morgan, word.

After experiencing the extremely high emotions of accomplishing the goal of being an actual student at Morgan State University, an enormous sense of loneliness swooped down over me like a thick heavy London fog. The isolation was overwhelming and daunting. I hadn't planned for or calculated these solitary new emotions; it was something that I had never experienced, feeling alone, far from home, and completely unknown.

My man Desi who was at my crib the day my mother gave me the boot, earned a full scholarship to play basketball for Morgan State. Desi had bionic, unbelievable hops and often monster-slammed dunked the basketball through the cylinder, leaving the capacity crowd in a wild uproar.

HISTORICALLY BLACK LOVE
The Golden Era

Desi played high school basketball for the powerhouse and nationally ranked Springfield Central High and was a teammate with the All-American Travis Best, who became a star point guard at Georgia Tech and played on several NBA teams.

Best played in the 2000 NBA Finals with the great Reggie Miller and the Indiana Pacers, coached by the legendary Larry Bird. The Lakers were equipped with the Zen Master Phil Jackson and the dynamic dual Hall of Famers Shaq and Kobe. The Pacers lost to the Lakers 4-1. Springfield Central High won the Massachusetts Division I State Championship in '91.

In my senior year of 89-90, Trav scored a whopping 51 points on us; the following year, he dropped a mind-blowing 81 points on my high school, setting the high school scoring record in Massachusetts. You can still walk into any barbershop in Springfield, and heads are still reminiscing about that basketball game.

I played with Trav on Dunbar's Big Will Express teams, even though I didn't get much run. The team was something like an unofficial AAU team; we traveled on the weekends throughout the Northeast region, competing in tournaments and games in cities such as Boston, Providence, Worcester, Hartford, New Haven, Bridgeport, Yonkers, Harlem, and Brooklyn. Trav was a certified Blue Chip; with him on our team, we were confident we could compete and win on any basketball court we laced up our sneakers on,

HISTORICALLY BLACK LOVE
The Golden Era

Travis Best enhanced everybody's gameplay on the court. He was simply the best basketball team-mate and competitor I played with and against and witnessed as a spectator. He did whatever he wanted to do on the court; Best was official as they came.

Central High basketball games were the hottest ticket in town. Every gymnasium in Western Massachusetts was jammed packed to capacity to see him masterfully play the game. Multiple times the fire marshals refused to allow any more spectators in the buildings; they considered the oversized crowds a health hazard.

One afternoon Travis asked me for a ride from the local hangout spot of Burger King on State Street. I wanted to assist Trav, but at that time, I was dabbling in the streets and was riding dirty, about to make a delivery; I couldn't take the chance of exposing him to a possible bad situation.

At that time, Best was a Five Star All-American and was heavily recruited by every major basketball program in the country, something like how Jesus Shuttleworth was being recruited in the Spike Lee joint, *He Got Game*, with superstar Ray Allen, in which Travis played a role in the film. Best was so nice; on the strength of his fan fair and national popularity, he brought the *McDonald's All-America Game* downtown to the Springfield Civic Center in 91. Future NBA stars Chris Webber, Jalen Rose, Glen Robinson, and Juwan Howard all played in the all-star high school basketball game.

Best might have thought I hated on him, but I didn't. I was one of his biggest fans and wanted him to succeed at all costs; I couldn't afford to put him in such a compromising situation. Around that time, Five-Stars recruits Allen Iverson and Randy Moss both got entangled in off-court controversies and every athletic scholarship offered to them from the nation's top programs was quickly relinquished. I couldn't take the risk of allowing Trav in the vehicle; the pressure was too heavy.

I had plans to link up with Desi when I got all my business situated at Morgan, but Desi and several other basketball players were suspended from Morgan's team just a few weeks before I arrived.

The basketball team got into a serious physical brawl with South Carolina State University during a televised game on ESPN. It was straight mayhem, wild and crazy. Each team member threw punches, water bottles, and chairs on national television. To my dismay, Desi transferred to a Connecticut school to play basketball after the fight.

The following Fall semester, our dormitory, The New Building won the intramurals championship; Coach Ramage invited me to work out with the basketball team after my stand-out performance and lock-down defense. I always wondered if Desi and I played together for Morgan; I believe we could have made some noise in the Mid-Eastern Atlantic Conference. With no Desi on campus, I was alone; therefore, I had to do my dirt all by my lonesome.

I was entirely on my own for the first time in my entire life. It was quite an uncomfortable position to find myself in. I seriously considered if I could manage this situation. I knew no one on campus or in the city of Baltimore. It was as if I was on the planet Saturn; everything was new, foreign, and strange to me. I pondered how I was going to maintain, survive and succeed in this environment. I began to seriously consider did I make an error and chose the wrong college.

Walking across campus, I saw many people and faces that reminded me of somebody from home by their mannerisms and how they walked, talked, smiled, and dressed. Still, the weirdest thing was I didn't know anyone, and no one knew me. It was a strange déjà vu feeling of being alone and homesick.

The loneliness was extreme, hundreds of students surrounded me, but I felt so alone. Maybe I should have stayed closer to home and taken the scholarship to Hampshire College offered to me by the attorney Art Serota and his organization, *The Learning Tree,* or gone to the University of Massachusetts. I was so unsure of myself and my situation that all I could do was activate my faith, bow my head, and pray to the Creator to help me find my way.

Every shade of tan, brown, and black skin represented the sea of students moving across the landscape. My keen senses were on overload, trying to process as much information about my new reality and environment.

I was now starting over from scratch in my new Black world. It was a difficult and uncomfortable transition to manage at that time. A couple of months ago, I was commuting to a community college in Massachusetts, where I stood out as one of the few Black males on campus and in class, I experienced many micro aggressions daily, mainly because of my Hip-Hop appearance of jeans, flashy sneakers, and baseball hats I often sported, My culture offended some folks.

HISTORICALLY BLACK LOVE
The Golden Era

The Rodney King incident in 92, when four police officers were acquitted after they gruesomely beat King within inches of his life, was caught on video. The racial tensions across the country and on the community college's campus were thick and heavy. As I was heading to my Sociology class, a mounted television in Building Nineteen was showing the riots burning down Los Angeles. This white dude and his buddy were walking closely behind me, having a conversation about the trial and the riots. I heard him say in a racist tone and hateful vibe, "He deserved the beating; the dude was resisting arrest and fighting the cops back.". It took everything in my power not to respond and knock this ignorant motherfucker out.

Now suddenly, everyone in my entire environment is primarily shades of beautiful brown skin. I wasn't as on guard, and quick to defend and protect myself; many of the students looked and dressed similarly to me. Off the bat, I noticed the many different styles and textures of hair the students wore proudly. Afros, dreads, braids, fades, waves, baldies, perms, and naturals, long and short hair, the observation helped me feel like I belonged and not an outcast. I'm now effortlessly blending in with various Black students, cohabitating in the dorms, and attending classes. Even in the cafeteria, the food served catered to a traditional African American diet. Seasoned fried chicken, fish, mac & cheese, collard greens, peach cobbler, and the like. In this strange, unfamiliar domain. I was experiencing some culture shock, to say the least; almost everybody was Black.

One of the initial and most important observations I made in this new world was all Black folks were not cut from the same cloth. African Americans are a rich, diverse pool of people with various perspectives, beliefs, and values, such as politics, religion, and social concerns and issues. Black folks stretch across the financial spectrum in the United States, some of us are very well off, and many of us are struggling just to get by, as was reflected on Morgan's campus.

Where you lived and were raised often determined your styles and culture; your speech patterns, geographical accents, rhythms, and pace were different.

While moving across campus heading to class, I keenly listened and observed the many tones, dialects, accents, and geographical slang terms or Ebonics and noticed how foreign they sounded.

Some words I'd never even heard before. For example, I had never heard the term *Bama* used and didn't know what it meant until my roommate D-Ray who was from Prince George's County, broke it down. A *Bama* is considered a lame, underachiever, or whack individual and is commonly used by D.C., Prince George County, and Virginia folks.

I always knew Black people were an assorted and diverse race, but the diversity was greatly illuminated on Morgan's campus and made an impression on me. I had to maintain and find my lane.

The second most obvious thing I observed about emerging in Black college culture is that everybody seemed to be rocking some name-brand label. The pressure to wear the latest fashions was worse than in high school.

HISTORICALLY BLACK LOVE
The Golden Era

You were considered suspect if you weren't wearing the latest name brands. It felt like being on the set of a Hip Hop music video set every day. The pressure to sport Polo, Ralph Lauren, Tommy Hilfiger, Nautica, N.Y.D.K., Liz Claiborne, Sean John, FUBU, Karl Kani, Phat Pharm, Rocka Wear, Timberland, Nike, Adidas, Champion, Guess, Levi's, and any other name brand labels played a significant role in first- and second-year students' lives.

If you endured and made it to your junior year, the illusion of labels, focusing on fashion, and stunting hard fades away. The primary focus is on studying, passing classes, and earning a degree. When the pressure is on, you could go a couple of weeks wearing the same pair of jeans and neglect your hygiene and every other aspect of your Life just to pass that one class.

I could quickly identify what geographical region many students represented by their fashion and how they wore them. The New Jersians, New Yorkers, Connecticut, and the "Up Top" folks had a distinct style.

They mainly sported colorful Nike Airs, Jordans, and tan Timberland boots. The big baggy jeans, Polos, athletic jerseys, leather jackets, and fitted baseball caps were the basic uniform for the Northeasterners. Many females from up top rocked the golden knocker, bamboo, or hoop earrings with their hairdos always impeccable.

Baltimore and D.C.ers had their original flavor too. Many rocked heavy double, extra-large thick, rich cotton grey or black sweatpants n by double and triple, extra-large white or black t-shirts, and fresh, crisp New Balance sneakers or tan Tim's. They also had this thing for simultaneously wearing at least three or four tube socks pulled up past their calves.

If you're watching a basketball game on television and the player's socks are pulled up to their knees, it is a good chance that the player is from the *DMV*, or D.C., Virginia, and Maryland areas. D.C. cats also had this distinctive style in which they bent the brim of their baseball caps up toward the sky.

The Philly folks were a mixture of Up Top, D.C., and Maryland areas; they had a little bit of everybody's flavor but maintained their original flow. The Philly dudes were serious about their three-quarter-length leathers. It seemed like every Philly brother rocked a long leather coat with crips tan Timberland boots, a Skully hat, and a nice, trimmed beard. Whether long and bushy or short, clean, and crisp, the beard game was serious and a part of Illiladelphia's culture. The Philly females had distinctive southern girl sweetness but don't consider their kindness a weakness. You don't want to get on their bad side; they had plenty of gangsta.

The other thing I keenly became aware of was that Morgan was a party school. Every day, somewhere on campus, was a party, get-together, or a reason to celebrate.

In my initial semester at Morgan, I almost lost my mind chasing after all the females and what seemed like endless parties popping up on and off campus. I was crashing every party I could, barely studying and struggling to get up for class. God forbid if you had a roommate who had a high propensity to party, too; it only made things more challenging to get up in the mornings or not fail out of school.

Greek Life played a substantial role in HBCUs. Morgan's beautiful, manicured landscape was peppered with the bright colors of letters and symbols of Greek Life. You often heard the catcalls and responses of "Skeet! Skeet!" or "Roof! Roof!" from the many members of the different sororities and fraternities. Communicating across campus in this manner was common and could be heard day and night.

The Divine Nine of the black Greek fraternities— Alpha Kappa Alpha, Alpha Phi Alpha, Kappa Alpha Psi, Delta Sigma Theta, Omega Psi Phi, Psi Beta Sigma, Zeta Phi Beta, Sigma Rho, Iota Phi Theta—all had a substantial presence on the black institution. The G.Q.' 's, Gentlemen of Quality was also a fraternal organization on campus but was not Greek-affiliated.

The primary purpose of Greek organizations was to develop and improve the individual and the Black race. They also were a great way to establish bonds, friendships, and relationships. A commitment to the organization was necessary and could take up to three months to an entire year to crossover and become a chapter member. Enormous amounts of time and energy were invested in learning and understanding their chapter's history, philosophy, and purpose.

An essential aspect of the pledging process was assigning each candidate a nickname. They had t-shirts in their organization's colors with their handles printed on the back, reflecting something about their personalities or history. Too Tall, Wet Dream, Bug Out, Stix, and Albert Einstein, just to name a few.

The fraternities and sororities would click up, assemble, and practice their step routines on beautiful afternoons sprinkled across the campus. At the same time, groups of students curiously gathered around and observed eagerly.

Crossing over, the day a candidate becomes an official chapter member of a Greek organization was a monumental and festive event or rights-of-passage. Steeped in decades of traditions passed down from the Founders was a serious responsibility, consisting of prestige and honor. Crossing over was a special moment for the individual and something they will cherish for the rest of their lives. Witnessing the crossover ceremony inspired many others to consider pledging to a particular fraternity or sorority.

Some organizations crossed over in the yard during the day, and others at midnight. It was a spiritual event with a rich tradition of recognizing the ancestors that came before them. Crossing over was a personal, spiritual journey.

During Homecoming Week, Greek Life took over the entire Morgan Campus. The Greek colors and symbols stood out in the sea of blue and orange. With all the fan fair of the highly anticipated step show contest between the fraternities and sorties in the Hill Field House, the parade down Hillen Road, and the football game, Morgan's entire campus was saturated with alums from decades back, representing Greek Life with its colors and symbols. It was also nice to witness the younger Greeks bond and pay homage and honor their elder brothers and sisters,

HISTORICALLY BLACK LOVE
The Golden Era

Throughout the semesters, in the middle of the crowded refectory, an athletic contest, a jammed-packed rocking party, or any other highly attended social event, potential candidates engaged in different rituals as part of their initiation process.

For example, the sores or frats were instructed to stand completely still in the middle of the live activity and not communicate, move, or respond in any manner, nor make eye contact for several hours with anyone in the environment.

I tried spitting my most deadly game at a potential Delta standing online and engaged in a discipline test at one of those parties. This tall, coco-brown female was wearing a red baseball cap low, her ponytail hanging out of the back of it. This female was super bad, the finest standing online. Wet-Wet was the name on the back of her shirt. I wanted to test my game and was confident enough to think I had enough swag to stimulate at least a tiny smile, eye contact, or slight laughter. My objective was to break her focus.

I pushed up on her strong and hard with my best game face on while she was standing at the end of the line with her eight other linemates during the jam-rocking party. I didn't touch her but got close as possible; wet-wet didn't budge or respond to my words. Throughout the night, I kept returning to the sexy potential Delta with my best Napalm Bomb lines to get into her mind, telling her how fine she was and what I would do to her if she were mine. I was close to her ear like headphones, but Shorty wasn't feeling me, and nothing I was saying to her. She was as strong as a bull and gave me no rhythm or response. I left the party feeling defeated like I needed to brush up on my game; in reality, Wet-Wet was determined to be a Delta.

HISTORICALLY BLACK LOVE
The Golden Era

Potential frats and sores were often heard to have done the wildest, craziest, off-the-wall antics to be a part of the brother or sisterhood. They were not permitted to disclose any of their experiences or the secrets of their organizations. Greek Life played a substantial role on Morgan's campus.

About two months into my new Morgan experience, a popular sophomore was stabbed and killed at a party. The sad and traumatizing situation shook the whole campus.

The ordeal affected me in such a way, even though I didn't know the young man. Seeing the pain and feeling the extreme grief on the faces of his friends and classmates made a lasting impression on me.

A grand tribute celebrating the fallen Morganite's Life was held in Murphy's Auditorium. His colleagues and close friends spoke on his behalf; it was a tragic event.

I thought I would be insulated from the world's ills on a university's campus, but the Illmatic aspects of Life always seemed to follow. I had to stay alert, even on campus. Sleep is the cousin of Death.

I made other vital observations and comparisons between the community college and the historically Black institution. Both had comfortable, attractive, sprawling campuses. The classrooms were equipped with the latest technologies and were moderate in size. The interactions between the professors, administrators, and staff were quite different at each school, though.

54

HISTORICALLY BLACK LOVE
The Golden Era

At Springfield Technical Community College, the instructors were constant professionals and experts in their subjects. They did an exceptional job of teaching what was needed to learn the subject and pass the course; it was all business. I don't recall establishing any bonds or relationships or remembering any of the professors' names, although my advisor at S.T.C.C., Mrs. Randell, was heaven-sent.

Mrs. Randell, a tall, redhead, blue-eyed white woman in an interracial marriage, guided, nurtured, and advised me throughout my S.T.C.C. journey and helped me transfer to Morgan State.

Mrs. Randall presented me with the indispensable gift of the Autobiography of Malcolm X and instructed me to "read the entire book!". X's manuscript was my blueprint and the genesis of my striving to be a scholar. If Malcolm could convert his thorny life into something constructive and positive, then I could too. Mrs. Randall was very important in my quest to me being a student at Morgan.

At Morgan, the interactions with many of the professors and administrators were warm and felt sincere. They were vested in our personal growth and development. The relationship between the lecturers and the student body was built on a family dynamic.

The Morgan staff left you with the impression they wanted to see you succeed and earn your degree. They advised us with words of wisdom and guided us without holding our hands. Many of the professors came from a genuine place recognized and respected. They spoke to us with sincere concern in their voices and hearts and

55

dropped jewels or words of wisdom on us. It was like your aunt or uncle advising or hitting you off with unique insight or information.

The culture of the staff and professors felt sincere like they had a personal stake in assisting us to be successful students. They understood how important it was to learn and earn a degree.

One semester at Morgan, I procrastinated on submitting my housing paperwork on time. Classes started the next day; I had no place to rest my head on campus or in Baltimore.

I carefully explained my dire circumstances to the resident director of the off-campus Northwood Apartments. He could have been my older brother or uncle. He had that cool, humorous, protective vibe, always looking out for the student's best interests. He seriously begins to inspect and study me, checking me up and down, searching for any sense of integrity. He gazed intensely into my eyes, meditating on me and my vigor for a good minute, trying to determine what he was going to do with me and my pressing situation. I was so nervous and vulnerable; this could be the end of my college career, and even worst, I could be homeless on the unforgiving streets of Baltimore. Everything was on the line based on this man's decision; he held the keys to my future.

Like I was now obligated to assist another brother in need, he then stated to me,

"Pass it on, young king."

HISTORICALLY BLACK LOVE
The Golden Era

He handed me a set of keys to an apartment; I wasn't charged that semester for housing. He recognized something worthy within me and afforded me some Black privilege. I sincerely thanked him, shook his hand firmly, and breathed a heavy sigh of relief. I'm not sure anyone at those white institutions would have given me such an immense pass.

I've always remembered the kind gesture of the resident director; whenever someone is in a pressing situation, and I can help them, I remember his words, "Pass it on, young king," and do my best to assist the individual.

During my second semester at Morgan, I gained a new and profound perspective on school and my education during my Freshmen Orientation class. Ms. Brooks, a former Morganite who was now employed as a student counselor for the institution, conducted a simple but effective exercise about the reality of being a student at Morgan.

I was slumped in the back of the class, wearing a Howard University African American College Alliance hoodie, recovering from parting heavy the previous night. When Brooks entered the classroom, she had the grace and presents of an ancient Egyptian queen. Her positive energy illuminated the contemporary McKeldin Center classroom; I instantly popped up; she had my undivided attention.

Ms. Brooks was naturally beautiful with these long, twisted locks that profoundly attracted me. I relocated to the front of the lecture hall sensing Ms. Brooks was essential; I needed to pay attention to her and her words.

HISTORICALLY BLACK LOVE
The Golden Era

The class was about 50 first- and second-year students from all social, academic, and regional backgrounds. The course's primary objective was to help all incoming students get acclimated to the university and help with useful information and resources, such as counseling, tutoring, and health needs, to help us navigate the black college experience.

Ms. Brooks instructed us to do the Thurgood Marshall exercise during the lecture.

"Look at the person sitting to the right of you."

She instructed.

"Now, look at the person sitting to the left of you. You must comprehend the statistics indicating the person sitting on either side of you will not be a student here at this institution next semester; fifty percent of you will drop out of college."

Her words were a sobering reality; I knew it could easily be me, a student who would not return. I struggled to make it to the class that morning from partying the night before; I was getting dangerously closer to the ledge. The social and academic pressures were mounting; I was either going to sink or swim at some point.

The following semester the words of Ms. Brooks rang true; half of the students from that lecture were no longer seen attending class or on campus; they became college dropouts. That class and Ms.

HISTORICALLY BLACK LOVE
The Golden Era

Brooks' penetrating words forced me to seriously contemplate all I'd endured to be a student at Morgan and what it would take to succeed.

6 That College Life

During the Fall semester of 95, on October 3, OJ Simpson was found not guilty of the murders of Nicole Brown and Ronald Goldman, a day on campus that will live in infamy.

It was around eleven in the morning, during the mid-day break, between eleven to one o'clock in the afternoon. This was the time when the students went to lunch, caught up on their studies, got some additional rest, and when the females jetted to their dorms to tune into the enormously popular Ricki Lake show.

I was behind six or seven of the fifteen heads waiting to get our hair cut by Low-Low, a dude from Philly who had masterful skills with the Clippers. It seemed every brother on campus chased Low-Low down for his impeccable grooming services during the mid-afternoon break. His Argonne suite was always packed around this time. He had you looking fresh to def and feeling like a million bucks for only ten dollars.

The television was on with the verdict about to be announced. I hadn't been paying much attention to the national trial, but from the little I watched, I thought O.J. was guilty. With the blood drops on the white Bronco, the cut on his finger, and catching a flight out of town soon after the murders were committed, I figured he didn't have a snowball's chance in Hell to go free. With all the facts stacked against him, I still didn't want to see the Juice convicted and go to jail.

HISTORICALLY BLACK LOVE
The Golden Era

The reading of the verdicts seemed to be happening so quickly that it was barely anytime to prepare for what was about to go down. All of us were glued to the television, and everyone got silent as the verdict was about to be announced; you could hear a pin drop; it was so quiet. We all knew the jury was going to convict the once-great Heisman Trophy winner and N.F.L. superstar running back. The only hope we clanged on to was the words from Simpson's Dream Team attorney, Jonnie Cochran, *"If the glove doesn't fit, then you must acquit."*

When the jury forewoman read off the verdict, we all lost our minds. It was such a shock to hear the words, *"Not guilty"* We all were in complete disbelief. The entire campus response to the verdict was spontaneous and organic. It was as if a nuclear bomb exploded in the middle of the university. Instinctively everybody rushed outside and spread across the school's ground, caught up in the wild fit of uncontrolled hysteria of the moment.

It seemed like every student on campus headed toward the Bridge screaming, yelling, hugging, celebrating, and crying with elation and joy; Simpson was a free man.

It felt like out of all the injustice African Americans endured over the many centuries in this country; they finally got some deserved payback when O.J. was found not guilty.

The elation was unmeasurable. The Welcome Bridge was flooded from end to end, with students celebrating on cloud nine. Cars and other vehicles on Cold Springs Lane below bumped and honked

61

their horns nonstop throughout the afternoon. That was a wonderfully fantastic day to be a student at Morgan.

After all the hysteria died down and I tuned into the local Baltimore news, what transpired on Morgan's campus was the complete opposite at our cross-town rivals, Townson State University, a PWI. They were completely in disbelief and deflated when the verdict was read. You could see on their white faces the disgust and how upset, shocked, and angry they were by the verdict. Many of the Towson students could not understand how O.J. got off. I didn't receive a haircut from Low-Low that Afternoon.

At the beginning of the '94 winter semester, D.C. and Baltimore were shut down due to a snowstorm blanketing the Northeast. The school was locked down for an entire week. A gang of us were downstairs, sitting cramped in the lobby of the New Building, watching college basketball on ESPN. I was tripping because I recognized Derick Kellogg and Eger Padilla balling hard for the University of Massachusetts. I grew up competing and being teammates with them at the Dunbar, high school, and other leagues and tournaments around the city. Padilla went to Central, and Derick played for Cathedral High. I was proud of them both. They were playing basketball for a major Division I program on national television, and I had been a part of that basketball pedigree.

After watching the Umass basketball game, cabin fever began to kick in for many of us after being cramped up and locked down in the dorms for almost a week. Someone suggests a football game in the snow against O'Connor, the other male dormitory on the other side of the campus. The Resident Director of the New Building announced over the A.P. system all interested in playing tackle football against O.C. should be down in the lobby in 15 minutes.

HISTORICALLY BLACK LOVE
The Golden Era

The game was at night and next to the Soper Library. The only lights that illuminated the field were the somewhat dark walkway lights. The conditions were brutal, even from a New England perspective. The snow was hard, heavy, wet, and about a foot deep, with a coating of ice on top. It was difficult to walk, let alone run through the dense snow and maintain your balance. It was cold as the Arctic.

It was about thirty brave hearts dressed in layers of sweatpants, jeans, and hoodies. Several Morgan football players were on both the New Building and O'Connor's teams in the Ice Bowl. Neither team wanted to lose the game; the essence of fierce competition hovered over the iced-out field. Brothers were getting trucked, smashed, and plowed deep into the snow on every play. The spirit was extremely serious and intense. Plays were designed and executed with precision and strategy. There was stunting, blitzing, and going for the deep bomb.

That was a hell of an Ice Bowl. I do not recall which dorm were the victors, but I know we all were sore and frozen to our bones for a couple of days. The long cold trek back to our rooms was the worst and dreaded by all of us. That was some fun college shit.

On any given day, Life at Morgan was a whole vibe. This chill click of Philly girls in the apartment downstairs often clicked up with my crew and had movie night along with these grand smoke-out sessions.

Belly, Juice. House Party and Friday were our favorite movies we watched in heavy rotation. This evening, we elected to watch the cult classic Friday, starring Ice Cube and Chris Tucker. That was our shit.

During one part in the film, when Deebo is riding the squeaky beach cruiser towards Craig's house, Craig, Smoky, and Red realize he is coming and panic. They know Deebo is good for jacking folks for anything they are holding of value. They instinctively removed their watches, rings, jewelry, and other things to hide them from Deebo, except for Red; he decided to tuck his necklace under his shirt instead of removing it.

Coordinated with the film, everybody watching the movie removed our watches, rings, jewelry, and wallets, tucking them in and hiding them under the couch cushions as if we were in the motion picture. After Deebo jacks Red for the chain his grandmother gave him, he rides off on the beach cruiser. We all, in concert, mimic Craig and Smoky and retrieve our watches, rings, and items. Then we all bust out laughing. That was the Friday movie ritual every time that portion of the movie came on. We would then all pass out on the floor and, in the morning, struggle to class, fronting as we cope. Stunts, Blunts, and Hip-Hop were the days.

7 Born Day Celebration

One of the best, most memorable, wildest, and off-the-chain birthday celebrations I have ever had was with my Morgan crew: Steve, E-Dub, Ken, Clay Dog, and Big Gee; that day will go down in infamy.

My twenty-third birthday celebration commenced with a small social gathering of my crew and the Philly females who lived in the apartment downstairs from Ken and E-Dub in Northwood.

It was a small gathering of maybe twelve of us. The rituals of getting it in, drinking, and smoking good bud got the party started right. Shots of Henny and Crown Royal, amongst other alcohol tonics, were being served and sipped while several blunts steamed in heavy rotation. The vibe was chill and laid back, with no pressure from any angles. Everybody was just kicking it and enjoying the moment.

The latest Hip-Hop and R&B softly played in the background. My birthday must have fallen on a Thursday evening because Martin was playing on the television. We all were tripping and amazed by the fact in this episode of the hit-situational comedy, the dime piece Tisha Campbell, who plays Martin's girlfriend, Gina, was wearing the exact blue with orange letters in white trim Morgan State sweatshirt I was wearing that night on my birthday. My spirits, as well as the small congregation's, skyrocketed through the roof.

65

HISTORICALLY BLACK LOVE
The Golden Era

The coincidence was remarkable, to say the least, and made the night feel unique and memorable for all of us Morganites. Our historically Black university, Morgan State, was getting national shine and exposure during primetime.

Martin's show reflected our culture in an honest but humorous manner and was one of the most popular sitcoms in the mid-nineties. We were beaming with Morgan's pride and joy. The party got even more turned up, all the way up. MARTIN!!

Big Gee didn't indulge in drinking or smoking. He had the aspiration to work for the Federal Government as an F.B.I. or C.I.A. agent; therefore, he needed to stay clean, sober, and conscious of his surroundings. He was still cool and didn't kill our vibe, making him the perfect candidate for our designated driver.

Somehow, all six of us managed to pile into the "Space Shuttle; Steve's all-black with gold trim 89 Acura Integra two-door, it was the model equipped with the classic flip-up headlights. It was ridiculous and almost impossible how we crammed into the small whip, but somehow, we did.

Drunk as hell except for Gee, cruising through the streets of B-More, we all sang off-key to Wu-Tang Clan's Method Man lyrics. M-E-T-H-O-D-M-A-N! I'm sure we'd have received several moving citations if the Baltimore City police had pulled us over.

After barhopping to a few spots in the seedy Red-Light district, we elected to hit a strip bar on Baltimore Street for my birthday celebration.

HISTORICALLY BLACK LOVE
The Golden Era

The search protocol was serious and extensive to enter the strip club. We were instructed to remove our footwear, empty our pockets into a basin, move through the metal detectors, and receive an aggressive, heavy-handed pat-down.

While standing in the line of the lobby waiting to get frisked, a big cock-deasil bouncer staffing the entrance, along with several other bouncers who looked like they played for the Baltimore Ravens N.F.L. team, addressed me in a particular manner by saying,

"Homie, you look like an emcee about to bust a rhyme?"

It must have been how I wore the blue Yankee fitted low on my head, the double extra-large Morgan State sweatshirt with a white t-shirt, Levi's denim, and a crispy pair of Jordans that projected a Hip Hop impression. That Ice Cube, Boys in The Hood look.

I thought to myself, real recognize real, and cracked a drunken smile, licked my lips, and declared confidently,

'I am an emcee; I am Hip Hop."

Cock Deasil then hit me with a challenge and a proposal.

"If you can spit some bars on the spot and it's not whack, I'll let you and your boys in the club for free!"

HISTORICALLY BLACK LOVE
The Golden Era

I'd chuckled, cracked a sinister smile, contemplated his proposal for a quick second, looked at Clay Dog, and gave him the signal. Clay started to beatbox on the spot. I aggressively spit my sixteen I had ready, locked, and loaded. Steve, Ken, and E-Dub supported us with spontaneous adlibs.

Superman Dan, I spit real Hip Hop when I dismantle microphones with my lyrical bop. I know you figured that. You thought it would be whack until you paid attention to the lyrics and heard they were facts. Since standing on the block wearing thick striped socks, I fell in love with the music they called Hip Hop. I know you figured that, you thought the rhymes would be whack until I came to life on the mic and illuminated the track. I go. I flow, it's infinite, you know, anytime anyplace you're feeling my soul, I got my nigga Clay Dog, the infinite creator above, they are spreading out hate while Cock Deasil showing us love, letting me and my niggas, on my born day, free into the club...

We got applause from the other fellas waiting in line, Cock Deasil gave me a pound and a man-hug and allowed us to enter the strip club at no charge.

The strip club was massive and popping, with all kinds of stallions dancing on poles and giving lap dances to anyone who would make it rain. We were college students and not equipped to splurge too heavily; however, we were able to make it sprinkle to a degree, thoroughly enjoyed it, and were highly entertained by all the eye candy surrounding us. Texas Tea was the icing on the cake that night. I will never forget her and the seductive birthday lap dance she gave me.

HISTORICALLY BLACK LOVE
The Golden Era

E-Dub informed the D.J. we were celebrating my birthday. An announcement was made to the entire club, congratulating and wishing me the best on my born day. This OG player, who might have been a pimp by the looks of his expensive suit and several diamond rings he was showcasing, brought the crew a few rounds. We acknowledged the OG, raised our shot glasses in the air, made numerous toasts, then knocked them all back.

To my surprise, this stunningly super bad, hot stripper, Texas Tea, grabbed me by the hand and graciously escorted me up to the center stage. Texas Tea was tall, thick, honey-toned, and exquisite. The way her ponytails hung down under a rhinestone cowboy hat and the thigh-high stilettoes' boots she was wearing reminded me of a Dallas Cowboys cheerleader.

I didn't know what to expect. She gave me the wildest, most seductive raunchiest lap dance in history. I almost toppled off the stool I was sitting on when the exotic dancer performed a summersault flip, landing in my lap with her pussy in my face. It seemed every patron in the building went wild, screaming, yelling, and cheering me on. Shit was off the hook!!

After a wild and eventful birthday celebration with the boys at the Baltimore strip club, it was time to get our eat on. The munchies were starting to kick in with the seriousness. We touched down at the IHOP, the popular breakfast spot after the club.

The bistro was beaming with activity and just as crowded as the club at four in the morning. There was a pancake promotion, and we consumed stacks and stacks of blueberry pancakes and several gallons of milk that morning.

We were sloppy drunk and began to flirt with a tribe of sisters sitting in the booth adjacent to us. They were cool, intelligent, and students at Coppin State, another historically Black College on the other side of Baltimore.

We pulled our tables together and engaged in some deep drunken spirited, current, social-political conversation and debate. I'm not sure it might have been about the OJ Simpson trial and how he got off, but the conversation got tense and heated.

The waitpersons approached our table several times, asking us to be considerate and mindful of the others trying to enjoy their meals. And could we please not be so disruptive and loud? We were hotheaded and having too good of a time.

The Shorty that attracted me from this click was a high-yellow, vanilla-flavored complexion cutie. She might have had some Asian in her ancestry because she had long, thick curly black hair and gorgeous, slanted hazel-green eyes. They had me in a trans. I was intoxicated and hypnotized by her specs and babbled and interjected about how they mesmerized my soul. I was getting on everybody sitting at the table's last nerve about how heavy I was sweating this female's eyes all morning.

My game was successful. I was able to pull Green Eyes to the side and have a private conversation. I learned she was from Maryland's Eastern Shore and was in school studying to become a Marine

HISTORICALLY BLACK LOVE
The Golden Era

Biologist. I got her information but misplaced it briefly on my way home. I don't recall her name, but I felt her and those eyes, damn, those hazel green eyes. Those eyes.

Being a kindred spirit and our savior that night, Big Gee returned us to Northwood unharmed. I wasn't in the condition to get up for my eight-thirty Chemistry lab, and mad Advil's were needed.

My twenty-third born day celebration was epic and legendary in every aspect. I will treasure that day as one of my grandest birthdays and Morgan experiences.

The small gathering set the night off in Northwood with the crew, the Philly girls, and the Morgan sweatshirt. How we all jammed in the Space Shuttle and rolled around B-more's streets, The freestyle Clay and I performed to gain access into the club, the wild and nasty lap dance I received from Texas Tea, breakfast at IHOP with the Coppin females at four in the AM and Green Eyes, was one of the most festive and entertaining nights of my life. Every young man should have one of those birthdays with his crew, especially if he is in college.

8 A First Time for Everything

The magical summer of ninety-five at the historically Black Morgan State University in Baltimore, Maryland, was special to me in more ways than one. I fell in love for the first time in my existence. As a young Hip-Hopper, I was transformed from trying to be a full-time player to falling head over heels for a Redbone I had just met from the Midwest. The situation was bugged and hit me like a ton of bricks.

Everything was genuinely overwhelming and happened so fast and fell perfectly into place. It felt like a dream to the greatest extent; it was difficult to fathom this was happening to me. I'm sure I would have never earned my bachelor's degree if she didn't come into my life. Like Superwoman, this Redbone swooped down and scooped me up just in the nick of time.

At that moment, love simply captured my heart wholly and instantly. I had nothing to do with the matter and couldn't deny it or resist; it was no use trying to. It was like I was captured in a net of love. The webby emotional mesh of love cast over my complete being nullified any doubts it was anything else.

I was a sophomore at a historically Black college—falling in love with any female was the last thing on my mind. Like most other HBCU college sophomores, I was living in the moment without a care in the world; the soundtrack of my days was Biggie's classic anthem: *Party and Bullshit*.

HISTORICALLY BLACK LOVE
The Golden Era

As a young man, falling in love for the first time was an overwhelming experience, especially when you're not ready, prepared, or have ever been exposed to real love.

I had fallen hard for a young lady for the first time. Until then, love was overrated and something to which I couldn't relate. Love was a manufactured emotion and could easily be discarded and effortlessly replaced.

Oh, how wrong I was until it happened to me. I never understood how anybody could be wholly infatuated with one person. It didn't make sense, but nothing you haven't felt makes sense until you experience it. There is always a first time for everything. It was my time and turn at Morgan in the summer of 95.

Falling in love with any female was the farthest thing from my reality; I didn't have the time, a dime, or a mature mind to hold down a steady relationship. Still, that's precisely what happened to me that summer. Cupid sucker-punched me into a whole new reality. It was simultaneously exciting, terrifying, and the most authentic sensation I'd ever experienced.

I was content to have just made it to Morgan State. It was the first and only college I desired to attend. It was a great personal accomplishment to get to Morgan, considering where I come from and everything I'd endured. I was unfocused and didn't have a plan, goals, or a clear purpose. I just wanted to be a student at Morgan.

HISTORICALLY BLACK LOVE
The Golden Era

I wasn't completely lost or a knucklehead. I was keen, capable, intelligent, and had a knack for figuring out most things once I observed all the facts. But really, I was going nowhere fast, drifting across that campus with no real plan, purpose, or strategy for obtaining a solid education or even a degree. I was winging it, moving on instinct and vibes, hoping they would lead me in the right direction before time expired.

The consequences of partying six nights a week, hitting every club in Baltimore, and neglecting my studies in all my classes approached; I was preparing for what I thought would be inevitable. I would have to withdraw from school. At that time, I couldn't envision myself draped in a cap and gown and participating in a graduation ceremony at Hughes Stadium.

The way I calculated things, by the end of the Fall semester, I was sure to be on academic probation. Then the following semester, it was over for me, lights out. I was losing my mojo. I didn't have the ambition or inspiration needed to earn a college degree. I was almost convinced I was concluding my educational endeavors.

My grade point average sank like a lead balloon. I transferred to Morgan State from Springfield Technical Community College in Massachusetts with a stellar 3.5 Grade Point Average. My G.P.A. steadily declined in each of the semesters I was at Morgan. By the summer of '95, it was at a dismal 1.6. The notion of doubt was starting to creep into my mind, and I began to believe that maybe I wasn't equipped with the necessary tools to manage this education experiment.

HISTORICALLY BLACK LOVE
The Golden Era

I was on the ledge and about to say, "fuck it', drop out of school, and search for gainful employment. I was resigned to the notion of having it on my resume. I attended Morgan State University for a few semesters and hoped for the best possible outcome. I was destined to be a college dropout.

Because of my procrastinating and constant partying, I hadn't taken the necessary time to plan accordingly for the summer—not an employment situation or even a residence to lay my head. I wasn't sure what the summer had in store for me. I was fearless, young, and somewhat irresponsible without a permanent residence in Baltimore. In my infinite wisdom, I neglected to plan to get back home to Massachusetts; basically, I was ass out.

By God's grace and presence, a summer work-study job opportunity instantly became available to me at the spring semester's conclusion. Special thanks to my country homeboy Levi, a Morgan middle linebacker from Kansas City, for showing me some love. He hooked me up and plugged me in with working for the campus Housing Department. The very next day, by 1230, I was obligated to be out of my dorm room and off-campus; I had no other options available.

The summer gig was a savior on many levels and worked out perfectly. It provided room, board, a stipend, and the opportunity to enroll in a couple of summer courses. Everything seamlessly and naturally fell into place that summer, including how Redbone came into my life.

Until Redbone entered the picture, I had no real idea why I was down at Morgan; my primary focus at that time was where is the party and who was rolling up the next blunt. Thank God for Redbone; she came just in the nick of time, and her love gave me purpose and direction.

This is my Historically Black Love, Golden Era, and Hip-Hop love story. Check it.

9 Fifty Grand, My Man!

The day I stumbled upon the likes of real love, I was chilling with my best friend at that time, OJ. I affectionately called him Fifty Grand because he always looked like he had money or came from wealth, even though he was always broke. Still, if I had the cash and O.J. needed it, he would be suitable for the dough.

Throughout my brief matriculation at Morgan, OJ and I became tight. We were road dogs, each other's wingmen, and held each other down at all costs; no matter the situation, O.J. and I were close comrades.

For a certified nerd, O.J. had some game. He could ball and had a competitive edge, which was one of the reasons I gravitated toward him and his style. He didn't possess much inside game—no post-up, big man moves, or the likes. However, he did have a deadly jumper in his arsenal and would often pull the trigger deep behind the arc. Once he got hot, it was lights out.

Fifty and I would often meet up by the Bridge, the popular gathering spot-on campus. We would go over there to post up, politic, check out some of the females, and then link up later at dinner, a ball game, a party, or whatever was on the agenda. He was a genuine person with a compassionate heart. I was glad Fifty and I were on the same team.

HISTORICALLY BLACK LOVE
The Golden Era

Our friendship was one of the few personal relationships I valued and actively cultivated at Morgan. O.J. was a sophomore pursuing a degree in Engineering; he was an intellectual and demonstrated nerdish qualities in a fast and alert New York style.

Fifty's philosophy was based strictly on quantifiable facts, information, and hardcore evidence. It didn't make sense to Fifty if it didn't add up. O.J. expanded my mind and taught me new and exciting things about science and life by providing me with an engineer's point of view.

He proudly represented Riverdale, an upper-middle-class neighborhood in the Bronx. His parents were professionals and Morgan alumni, graduating in the mid-seventies. His father was a prominent New York City Civil Engineer, while his mother was a tenured Philosophy professor at Columbia University. O.J. had the honor, privilege, and burden of carrying on the family tradition of continuing the Morgan legacy.

Fifty Grand's thesis revolved around this one device he talked so passionately about all the time. He desired to invent a specific type of hydraulic machine to revolutionize the mechanical industry and change the world. He spoke about it 24/7, attempting to illustrate how the mechanism was supposed to operate. He would draw sketches on pieces of paper, napkins, or anything he could get his hands on to try and better illustrate his point of view.

While I patiently and respectfully listened to him articulate his plans, I never fully understood much of the terms, engineering jargon, or scientific concepts he presented to me. Some of it was way beyond my comprehension and education.

HISTORICALLY BLACK LOVE
The Golden Era

You could never tell if O.J. was on his worst day because he was always dipped in the latest conservative fashions. Even though he resembled a young Michael Jordan—tall, slim, and brown-skinned, he was a Kanye West prep.

His wardrobe consisted of bright, colorful sweaters, button-downs, and Polos tucked into his neatly pressed khakis pants. He often rocked stylish, professional blazers or designer tweed sports coats. He wore polished wingtips, hard bottoms, penny loafers, or boat-type shoes complemented by a heavy sock game of crazy designs and colors. He often toted a brown, patent-leather briefcase with an over-the-shoulder strap to enhance his G.Q. swag.

I could prep it with a polo or button-down shirt, but I was no competition to Fifty. I knew my lane—a comfortable pair of 560's Levi's jeans, a crispy pair of Nikes, and a baseball cap, and I was straight. O.J. and I were culturally and intellectually from two different ecospheres.

He was a jazz lover; I was strictly a Hip-Hop head. Hip-Hop was my first true love before Redbone came into the picture. Nevertheless, we clicked and were on the same accord about numerous things, and basketball was one of those things.

The love for the game of basketball was the only matter we had in common. We'd discuss and debate the game of basketball and its rich history all day and night, from the college ranks to the pros. We often played on the same team whenever we ran pick-up ball in Hurst's Gymnasium. Our games complemented each other.

10 Northwood Plaza

It was a late, beautiful sunny Friday afternoon. Fifty Grand and I were window shopping in the plaza, the shopping center across the street from Morgan State University's campus. Northwood was a mid-sized plaza with several small mom-and-pop establishments and a few national chain stores.

The only grocery store in the plaza was a C-Town. Most Morganites would shop there if they didn't have the necessary transportation to jet up the parkway to other markets like Kroger's or Stop n' Shop. The C-Town was considered the "Ghetto Store" because their fruits, vegetables, and poultry quality was suspect or not the best.

One of our favorite establishments in the plaza was the Black-owned family business, Uptown Sounds. I'd purchased most of my Hip-Hop from Uptown. I wanted to support Black own businesses instead of spending my money at the big chain stores. *The Main Ingredient* by Pete Rock & CL Smooth, *Whut Da Album* by Redman, *ATLiens* by Outkast, and *The Stakes is High* by De La Soul are just some of the albums I copped at Uptown Sounds.

While Fifty was in the back of the store, flipping through their huge jazz vinyl collection, I checked for the latest Hip-Hop CDs up in the front. The rows of CDs were equipped with headphones so the customer could sample the music before they made a purchase. That afternoon I bought Tupac's third album, my favorite and critically acclaimed, *Me Against the World* masterpiece. Pac was locked in prison after being convicted in a sexual assault case. *Me Against The*

HISTORICALLY BLACK LOVE
The Golden Era

World soared to number one on the music charts while the poet was locked up in Clinton Correctional Facility, a maximum-security prison in upstate New York.

Northwood was also fortified with a small but popular live Jazz tavern called the Haven. I checked it out several times, but it wasn't conducive to my needs. The Haven catered to an older, more seasoned crowd. *It had a Mo Better Blues* vibe.

The plaza also had a Domino's Pizza and a barbershop, a Chinese food restaurant, a check-cashing spot, a hair supply store, a Marshall's, a Hechinger's Home improvement warehouse, and of course, a liquor store.

Classes were over, and Fifty and I decided to get our drink on with nothing but the weekend ahead of us. Fifty relished his whiskey and brought a pint-sized bottle of Old Granddad brandy. I purchased a 40-ounce of St. Ides malt liquor. I've never been a big-time drinker, but occasionally, I would get it in.

We settled under the cool shade of an elevated parking lot on the side of Hechinger's warehouse, facing Hillen Road, the southern end of Morgan's campus. We were tipsy, talking shit and philosophizing about life and our futures for about an hour. Fifty couldn't understand the fascination of drinking beer from a big ass bottle.

He growled at me in a heavy Bronx accent.

HISTORICALLY BLACK LOVE
The Golden Era

"Them bottles are so big the beer will be at room temperature by the time you finish it,"

"You must drink it fast and learn to enjoy the crisp, cold malt taste."

I casually responded, tilting the big, frosty bottle back and taking several long, satisfying gulps. And then let out a long disgusting burp and said,

"And you enjoy the way that nasty poison tastes?".

Dismissing my words, and took another quick swig from his bottle.

"It's an acquired taste." He replied.

The previous semester Fifty allowed me to take several shots of the Old Granddad. It was the nastiest. It was like gasoline mixed with rubbing alcohol—the disgusting taste left me with the worst throbbing headache I'd ever experienced. It felt like my head was going to explode. The hangover left me feeling like I was on the cusp of death, and I vowed never to drink Old Granddad again. I couldn't understand how he appreciated such a horrible, repulsive-tasting liquor.

After drinking, we returned to campus and got our grub on in the refractory. We were buzzing, and the steamy Baltimore sun was settling down.

HISTORICALLY BLACK LOVE
The Golden Era

Crossing the four busy lanes of Hillen Road took about five minutes and some change to reach the campus. We made our way around to the back of the New Building, my place of residence since I had transferred to Morgan three semesters ago. The dining hall was brand new, too and attached to the brand-new structure.

To provide some context, Morgan State was going through a significant transformation; the state had invested substantial amounts of capital in the renaissance of the historically Black institution. Many of its buildings were new or rehabilitated and equipped with modern upgrades and the latest technologies. The structure opened that spring semester and was called the New Building. The dormitory would later be named Rawlings Towers in honor of a Maryland Senator a couple of semesters later.

It was Friday, and the refectory was an event in itself, and it was sure to be live with females—an excellent way to start an adventurous weekend. During dinner time, you learn the intel to find out what's popping on campus, and in Baltimore, the shows, parties, and get-togethers all began in the refract.

11 Who's That Girl?

Fifty Grand and I patiently stood half-sozzled in the long, congested line stretched out into the hallway amongst the other summer school students waiting to be served dinner.

The menu was stacked and consisted of hamburgers, cheeseburgers, fries, all kinds of pizza, salads, pies, cakes, peach cobbler, and ice cream, along with fried and baked chicken and fish, collard greens, mac and cheese, black-eyed peas, potatoes salad, baked beans, okra, candy yams, and many other traditional soul food cuisines.

I scoped out the scene while the lines slowly moved into the cafeteria, my eyes locked in and focused on this short Redbone standing in the bar across from Fifty and me.

There was something about this Redbone. She strangely caught my undivided attention and stood out amongst all the other females standing in line with little effort. It wasn't anything blazing hot or appealing about her. She possessed an aura that was soft and sexy. It was a low-glow, cocoa kind of flow, which I'd immediately recognized.

The first thing that caught my attention was Shorty's hair. It was halfway pulled up; half of it was hanging down to her shoulder with two yellow pencils looking like Chinese chopsticks holding her hair together, giving off the impression that she was a serious academic. Her wig was thick, rich, and healthy. Even though it wasn't done in a particular style, you could easily see she invested plenty of time and attention into her tresses. Her hair looked like it smelled fresh, clean, and silky soft to the touch.

This light-skinned cutie stood a suitable 5'2 or 3; she wasn't too thick and not too skinny, with nice-sized, plump breasts and a slim waist. She was casually dressed in a white Morgan State t-shirt, navy blue, khaki shorts, and comfortable-looking white foam slippers adorned her pedicured toes. She was equipped with a nice pair of muscle-toned thighs, legs, and calves, the type that complemented any shoe game, be it heels, sandals, wedges, or sneakers. A large multi-colored striped bag was draped over her right shoulder.

Redbone wore a serious and unapproachable demeanor on her face while holding her tray in the line waiting to be served. She emitted a vibe that her day was long and enduring, and she just wanted to sit, relax, and have a bite to eat.

After studying Redbone's style for a brief time, I realized I didn't recognize this female and had never noticed her on campus. I pondered if she was a new student and, if so, where is she from and what's her name. My curiosity heightened, and my nostrils flared. I wondered, Who's that girl?

12 Playa Playa

I will be the first to admit—I was a dog, but a good dog, something like a Black Labrador Retriever, handsome, friendly, and curious, always on the prowl, sniffing around looking for something to get into. I lived for a different female each day of the week; I never considered settling down with any one girl, *especially* on Morgan's campus.

Before transferring and starting a new life in Baltimore, I was not claiming a title of a pimp by any means, but I was a certified playa. Since I was a five-year-old snotty nose, I was smitten by a pretty face. By the seventh grade at Forest Park Middle School, I was on my Bobby Brown and New Editions shit and began compiling a stable of young females.

As I matured throughout my adolescence, I began to home in on what I liked and was attracted to in a female. I gravitated toward intellect in a girl. They stimulated my mind and were more interesting than a female whose primary concern was what kind of whip I was pushing, how much bread was in my pockets, and whether I could break them off with the loot.

Intelligent girls were just more attractive to me; they knew different and exciting things, and their minds were more open to the possibilities of life. I like to learn and be in the know; I'd ask plenty of questions. That was a significant turn-on for me, a female fortified with facts and information that could expand and open my mind and educate me about things. Intelligent females were the best vice for me to learn and soak up knowledge from.

The ability to articulate precisely what you're thinking and feeling are qualities second to none. Intelligence is an asset; in a sense, it illuminates desirability. There is nothing sexier and more attractive than a beautiful female with the mind to complement her natural exquisiteness.

After this one basketball game during my junior year, everything seemed to change for me. It was the biggest game in the city, the Putnam Beavers versus the Central Golden Eagles. Central was a powerhouse and nationally ranked. This game was for city bragging rights; the pressure was on.

Central's gymnasium was jammed packed to capacity; anybody who was somebody in the city was at this game. The press, politicians, including the Mayor, Hood stars, drug dealers and playas, girls from every high school in the city, older seasoned, and the young at heart were all in the building to watch the high school basketball rivalry.

After this one basketball game, my life began to change on multiple levels. All kinds of opportunities and females began to manifest and were now available to me.

I also believe because of that one game, Ms. Satterwhite, the Executive Director of the Dunbar Community Center, who was in the bleachers of the big game, approached me and asked me if I was interested in attending college. After checking my report card, which was the first time in my life, I had decent grades, five B's and one C, second honors. Satterwhite made it her business to have Dunbar sponsor me to be a participant on the 89 Black College Tour. That game enabled a lot to happen, and I took full advantage of every opportunity afforded to me.

Halfway through the first quarter, I was activated off the bench and inserted into the exciting game to play ball with the big boys and make my presence felt. I knew college scouts would be at the game; my primary objective was to make a lasting impression.

I dropped eighteen points and snatched ten rebounds in the contest. I was in my zone, and hitting everything, I threw up. Deep high arcing jumpers, aggressively pulling down rebounds, drawing fouls, and hitting my free throws.

The enormous amount of pressure of being at the free throw line in front of a packed house, screaming, yelling, and going ballistics, was the most intimidating predicament I'd experienced. When I approached the free throw line after I received an aggressive foul by Fred Smith, a Central standout and a Dunbar product, the crowd began to rumble and stomp their feet, screaming my name at the top of their lungs; it sounded like a Kentucky thunderstorm was rolling through the gymnasium. I could feel the kinetic energy forcefully recoil through my body.

I wanted to tuck my tail and walk out of the gym, but instead, I fearlessly embraced the moment, relaxed, took a deep breath, focused my mind on my shooting technic, and hit both free throws, all net.

HISTORICALLY BLACK LOVE
The Golden Era

There was this one moment of that game I will always treasure. I hit a beautiful deep, high-arching jumper just inside the three-point line by the baseline. My feet and shoulders were squared up. The ball seemed like it touched the gym's ceiling, and rain dropped straight through the cylinder, nothing but all net. The capacity crowd on both Central and Putnam's sides rose to their feet and went crazy with applause. I left my arm extended in the air with my wrist in the fixed position as I gingerly back peddled down the sidelines, like I belonged on the court with the Central all-stars, soaking it all up.

Central defeated us by twelve points. I received a resounding standing ovation from the crowd when Coach Butler subbed me out of the game with two minutes remaining on the clock. That was one of the finest standout moments in my teenage years as an athlete. I felt honored, proud, and respected for my efforts as an athlete.

The only sour thing about that game, no one from my family was there to witness, support, and share that special moment with me. They never attended any of my football or basketball games, even though I was a standout varsity starter.

From that game on, my name Dan Coles was often mentioned in the local newspaper. I even had a large photo of me taking it to the hoop with my left hand plastered on the Sports section of the Union News front page. I brought a newspaper bundle and passed them out to anybody who would take them. I cherish that photograph to this day.

I also earned some respect amongst the community of official ballers in the city. At the Dunbar, where the best high school players congregated, my name was now amongst those getting respect; I was getting my props.

Folks I didn't know approached me on the streets, often complimented me on my gameplay and asked what college I planned to attend like I was being heavily recruited by colleges and universities. I only had one varsity start before that game; I made that type of impression.

From that point on, the females were coming out of the woodwork. From every high school in the city, girls began to check for me, pulling up on me, asking did I need a ride, or inviting me to hang out with them. I was now receiving free haircuts and could get into the parties at no cost. I was now invited to the exclusive skip parties, hanging out with the cool kids. Various girls, Blacks, Whites and Latinas, hood chicks, suburbans, and dime pieces were available to me.

While I was still in high school, I even scooped a couple of college girls from the local colleges; it was ridiculous; the girls were coming from everywhere.

When I reached the age of twenty-one, being in college was a personal requirement for all the females I was involved with. I wasn't wasting my time with any bird or chicken. I desired my females to be informed, educated, and able to put me on to new and different concepts and ideas. Nothing is worse or more unattractive than a fine female whose head is filled with helium. It's a major turn-off to me, a dumb girl.

HISTORICALLY BLACK LOVE
The Golden Era

I avoided females with children. It's not that I didn't adore children; I just refused to care for or babysit any child that wasn't mine. Plus, females with babies have too many needs, such as food, diapers, clothing, affection, attention, love, care, and money, which I was not about to forfeit to any female. I liked my girls to be spontaneous and free to be able to pick up and bounce out of town at a drop of a dime, with no worries or concerns.

On one of those spontaneous excursions, I bounced to New York City with a shorty. We ate lunch at the renowned soul food spot Sylvia's in Harlem and took in a New York Knicks basketball game at the world-famous Madison Square Garden. Pat Riley was coaching the Knicks, equipped with Sprewell, Ward, and Houston. They were playing the Orlando Magic with a young Shaq and Penny Hardaway.

During halftime, everybody in the World's Most Famous Arena eyes was glued to every television screen in the building. Magic Johnson, the great Los Angeles Lakers All-Star Guard, was wearing a black suit and tie and a daunting look of despair on his face. It was the moment he announced to the world he was H.I.V. positive.

I was shaken, confused, worried, and brokenhearted. One of my beloved basketball players and heroes had contracted the immune disease AIDS. Back then, having H.I.V. was a certified death sentence. I thought if Magic could get sick for not having safe sex, so could I. From then on, I was paranoid and never took a chance. I always was equipped with a fresh pack of Jimmy Hats.

HISTORICALLY BLACK LOVE
The Golden Era

I also preferred the natural kind of girl, with no make-up or weaves. A clown face never attracted me; I like to know what I am getting and can appreciate what God has given her.

I was chilling with a female I finally pulled after some time and effort were invested in the situation. I was attempting to be smooth and tried to run my fingers through what I thought was this female's long silky hair. I was hoodwinked. My fingers got stuck on a track, and the texture of her actual hair felt like an old rusty Brolo pad. I was horrified and felt bamboozled like a bait and switch was performed on me. Weaves and wigs are major turn-offs for me if they are not done correctly.

Being a survivor and a front-row witness to my nuclear family's atomic meltdown, watching everything fall apart into a heap of radioactive trash, I'm sure it affected my perception of commitment and marriage.

My parent's marriage of close to twenty years ended in the worst manner possible. They always argued and brutally fought; it's a miracle they didn't kill one another. I could hear my father's fist pound against my mother's flesh. It's one of the sickest sounds for a child to listen to, your mother getting beaten by your father.

To make things even worse, I watched my best friend's family go through a similar situation. Devastated and traumatized on multiple levels, marriage wasn't a good thing; they all seemed to end badly. I wasn't sure I believed in holy matrimony after what I observed and was exposed to when things went all bad.

HISTORICALLY BLACK LOVE
The Golden Era

I would never wish any child any of what I was exposed to and what I had to endure. My family dissolved into the Hunger Games; all my siblings went for themselves. Everybody was trying to hang on and survive the best we could. The wounds last a lifetime and affect every aspect of your life. I couldn't and wouldn't want to curse my babies in such an unforgiving and compromising manner.

After my parent's messy separation and devastating divorce, I vowed to myself I would never have any children with a woman with the same neglectful tendencies as my mother and never be like my father, a deadbeat that completely abandoned his babies, something I couldn't respect.

I was broken in many ways, watching my family fall apart. I'm still trying to heal and maintain from that event. Exchanging any vows and getting married, Nah, I couldn't see it.

I always assumed that if I did settle down and create a domestic situation, the mother of my seeds would have to be super superior, a one-of-a-kind, wholly devoted to our family and me, my soulmate, which I didn't believe she existed.

I was struggling with severe trust issues; I knew how trifling some females get down. Some of them have more game than some men and can look you dead in the eyes and lie.

I always compiled a mean *Starting Five* and had a few riding the bench. Not all my girls were about having a sexual conquest; each girl understood and played her role on the Coles squad.

HISTORICALLY BLACK LOVE
The Golden Era

Some of my females had solid culinary skills and would cook me a satisfying home-cooked meal from time to time. Others held me down, hitting me off with financial assistants, gear, and sneakers. Others were strictly for good times, and others were for stimulating conversation and companionship. I wasn't a whore slanging dick everywhere; I just appreciated beautiful, intelligent, attractive females.

The primary requirement I demanded from my girls was that they could teach and educate me about something I didn't know or understand. They all served a purpose in my life.

I was still adjusting on campus and had not compiled an active roster; I was still trying to find my lane. At this point, I had a few pieces, but nothing official or to brag about.

I was in college with no actual means to fund a committed relationship; I wasn't concerned about having a steady. I understood I was playing the numbers game; the odds were *always* in my favor. If I got shot down or was unsuccessful at trying to run game on a shorty, I wouldn't sweat it; it was all good. As Gucci Mane stated in one of his rhymes, like the bus, another is always coming.

I was learning how to sharpen my game to get into a female's head. I was heartless and knew how to control my emotions. My confidence and Mack game progressed to the point I felt that I could have any girl I wanted if I played my cards right. Settling down with one girl, I couldn't do it; there were too—many beautiful females worldwide and especially on the Morgan State University campus.

HISTORICALLY BLACK LOVE
The Golden Era

I still remember the morning during my first week as a student at Morgan when I was recovering from a hangover. The night before, I went to a party on campus and almost lost my mind drinking and smoking. I was wet, and I scooped the finest girl at the party. I didn't care and pushed up on her firm, setting the tone for the night. We hit it off the whole night. I was up on her close and didn't see anything wrong with a little bump and grind. To make things even more interesting, I was wearing sweatpants.

I felt this female and could feel the haters hating heavily, but I honestly wasn't concerned. This female was a straight-up dime, Aliya type, super bad. I later learned from my roommate the sexy thang I was kicking it with was Shelly, a Morgan cheerleader and the quarterback of the Morgan football team's main piece.

The following day after having a conversation with my roommate, he gave me the impression I should fall back from pushing up on the females too strongly straight out the gate; I might be violating some "*Other Person's Property.*" Although I'm sure, my roommate was hating.

The historically Black university was saturated with beautiful females. My classes always had at least a dollar's worth of certified dimes. I felt like a prince surrounded by the best. The female-to-male ratio was something like 21-1. A young man could seriously lose his mind with the amount and variety of females on campus; they came in all shapes, sizes, and shades of brown from every corner of the globe. All kinds of minds and intellects were right there at my fingertips. It didn't matter if it was in class, on campus, day, or night. Every day was better than being at any club on a Friday

HISTORICALLY BLACK LOVE
The Golden Era

night in Massachusetts. Finding an attractive brown skin woman was never an issue. The queen bees could rock sweatpants and a hoodie to class and still command respect and attention.

I learned to appreciate and respect a woman's mind on that campus. Despite her physical attributes, you can often have a stimulating, intellectual conversation with a woman. I grew comfortable in an environment condensed with beautiful, intelligent, strong, Black women. Interacting with women of a high caliber enhances a man's confidence on many levels. You become fearless and accept all challenges.

Morgan had plenty of high-quality women but don't get it twisted; there were plenty of chicken heads clucking on campus too. Some females didn't have a clue or even know why they were even in school. They were beautiful and had no brains. Those types didn't last long, maybe a semester or two.

The Welcome Bridge is where it all went down every Thursday at around twelve. It was a tradition and a ritual for us, fellas, to post up on the benches in front of the Soper Library, Cummings House, or the McKellen Center to watch the show go by. It was as if a full-blown, high-end fashion show was taking place on the North Campus, and crossing the Bridge was the primary catwalk for the Morganites models.

The pressure was heavy. It was as if the females prepared for and competed against one another to see who was the fiercest on campus that week. We'd evaluate the females as super-models; we were the adjudicators tasked with judging their hairdos, outfits, and shoes.

HISTORICALLY BLACK LOVE
The Golden Era

Oh, my goodness, you had to be there on those Thursday afternoons by the Bridge to understand and appreciate how truly and focused these females were trying to grasp the Queen Bee status for that week. It was like being at a mini-Freak-Nik for a couple of hours. Beautiful brown, young females dressed to the t everywhere; it was a sight to see and a player's playground.

For those who don't know, the *Freak-Nik* was the destination spot for HBCUs during Spring break in the early '90s in Atlanta, Georgia. Thousands of young African American college students flocked to the ATL and partied in the streets all week long; it was the ultimate block party.

That summer, even though I was on shaky grounds academically, I was starting to find my lane socially on the historically Black college campus and in the city of Baltimore. I was about to spread my wings; *I* never considered I would want to settle down with one female on campus, and then I met her, Redbone. She rocked my world.

13 The Introduction

Fifty Grand and I received our dinner and began navigating the crowded dining hall. Off instinct or reflex, I calculated passing directly in front of the Redbone to exchange energy to stimulate any response.

"That's a healthy and nutritious-looking meal,"

I shot off the head at Redbone as I glanced at the food on her dinner tray. This cutie's meal consisted of yellow rice, crispy green broccoli, a scoop of mashed potatoes with gravy, and a small portion of pink salmon.

From my lyrics, Shorty became animated and brightened up, flirtatiously responding by saying,

"I try!"

She flashed her gleaming smile and sauntered off in front of me into the cafeteria. At that moment, the chase was on.

Fifty Grand and I secured some decent seats in the regionally segregated, cliqued-out dining hall. The football players and other Morgan athletes huddled at the tables in the back by the exit doors. You could easily distinguish the athletes by the blue and orange

HISTORICALLY BLACK LOVE
The Golden Era

athletic gear they usually sported. The New Yorkers and Jersey's heads congregated and socialized together, as did the Philly, B-More, D.C., and Prince George County students. The Greek organizations had their designated tables too. The Iota's, Kappa's, Zeta's, and others comingled together. The rest of us were sprinkled throughout the new dining facility. Multiple layers of conversations competed with silverware clanging against ceramic plates while the latest Bad Boy music thumped in the background. The festive environment set the tone for the weekend on campus.

While we sat at an open table and began to scarf down our dinner, I located the short Redbone on the other side of the cafeteria, sitting by herself. I asked Fifty for his opinion on how Shorty looked and her vibe.

"Yo, what do you think of that female over there by herself? The short Redbone sitting by the window, how does she look?"

Without the benefit of my contact lenses, I couldn't embellish the fine details from that distance.

"Shorty is right, Son."

Fifty Grand co-signed my suspicions, indicating she was a dime from his perspective.

"Yeah, Shorty is official, no doubt."

HISTORICALLY BLACK LOVE
The Golden Era

Off the strength of Fifty's co-signature, it put the battery in my back to go over to where she was sitting and introduce myself. At the least, I would get her name. The forty of St. Ides I'd consumed earlier at Northwood had something to do with my bold confidence.

Anticipating conversation, I brought my plate of fried chicken, mac and cheese, collard greens, and candy yams across the canteen to where Redbone was sitting. She saw me approaching her and unconsciously brushed a bang of her hair to the side as though she was anticipating or preparing for some interaction. I stopped directly in front of where she was sitting and said with confidence.

"You look lonely,"

"I may look lonely,"

she quickly responded in a Mid-Western twang, slightly rolling her neck, peppered with a hint of attitude.

"Trust and believe I am not alone."

I cut right to the chase while making a gesture with my plate,

"Do you mind if I sat and joined you?"

she responded in a quick, sarcastic manner.

HISTORICALLY BLACK LOVE
The Golden Era

"The last I checked, this is a free country."

I chuckled and thought to myself this is going to be an interesting conversation as I took the seat across from her.

I attempted to ask her name.

"Hi, my name is Danny, but my friends call me Coli. It's nice to meet you—"

She jumped in and interjected, asking,

"Is it Dan, Dannell, or do you prefer Danny?"

"I prefer Danny or, Superman-Dan, but you can call me Coli. Either or is alright with me."

"I see your confident; that's good, Superman-Dan. Why do your friends call you Coli?"

"Because my government last name is Coles, C-O-L-E-S, my peoples call me Coli for short. What do your folks call you? What is your government name?"

I'd inquired.

HISTORICALLY BLACK LOVE
The Golden Era

Her name sounded unique, like her voice, proper with a slight Mid-Western twang. It was not anything ethnic or ghetto; it was different.

"I have never heard that name before."

I admitted.

"It's original. Does it have any special meaning?"

"Yes, it does. I'm my parent's third lovechild, so they thought the name would be appropriate, so that's how my name was bestowed or given to me."

"Wow, such a beautiful thing, an authentic lovechild. What an honor to be in your presence."

She seemed impressed that I even understood the significands of a lovechild and its implication. I got her attention.

"You must be studying to become an attorney with all that attitude," I teased.

"No,"

she replied matter-of-factly.

HISTORICALLY BLACK LOVE
The Golden Era

"I will shape the minds of the future. I'm studying to become an educator."

"A teacher, that's a noble profession. It takes a special individual to take on such an awesome responsibility."

"I *am* special."

"I bet you are."

"Do you always carry a plate of fried chicken with you when you meet a female?"

She smirked.

"Only if she is equipped with a certain gravitational pull."

Redbone flashed her beautiful smile. I then asked her one crucial question most brothers seek to know about females on campus.

"Do you have any cooking skills; can you get down in the kitchen? Nothing is more satisfying than a home-cooked meal when you're far away from home?"

"I have some culinary skills in the kitchen; I can burn a little," she pompously replied.

Off the strength of her distinct accent, I asked her where she was from. It was one of my go-to lines; I used it often to help reel in the females. I was genuinely curious, though; she had a distinctive sounding drawl; it sounded familiar.

While waving air quotes with her hands, Redbone said.

"I represent a suburb north of the Windy City of Chicago, Chi-Town."

In some way, I was relieved by that information, considering that most of the females on campus were from the New York, Jersey, Maryland, and V.A. areas. This meant a young man such as myself had to contend and endure the East Coast sassiness and high maintenance attitudes more likely than not. At that time, I wasn't fully equipped to manage those situations.

Her twang brought me back to my days growing up in Kentucky during my early adolescence; it reminded me of someone or someplace I once knew.

I truly sensed something special; the Magic was present from the beginning. The chemistry was intense and undeniable. I knew she was different from the rest with her quick wit and intelligent dry sense of humor.

HISTORICALLY BLACK LOVE
The Golden Era

Redbone and I were fully engaged as we chatted about this and that. In the 20 minutes, we kicked it. Our conversation flowed strongly and effortlessly with vigor and zest. I felt unusually comfortable and relaxed in her presence in the short time we were getting acquainted. It was a different kind of feeling, a different kind of vibe.

Our subject content expanded around the globe and back. We laughed, cracked a few jokes, touched on political issues, and discussed current events.

She wasn't a bird; Shorty could hold her own. She was knowledgeable and well aware of what was happening in the world.

It felt like we were old friends, reengaged and catching up on things like we knew each other from a past relationship or life. The banter was far from what I had expected; I was pleased and pleasantly surprised.

I asked Redbone, "*Chi-Town*," where she was residing on campus. She reached into her bag, retrieved a ballpoint pen, scribbled something down on a paper napkin, and handed it to me. To my surprise, it was her campus address.

"If you're in my neck of the woods, don't be a stranger. Stop by and say hi."

Redbone smiled.

HISTORICALLY BLACK LOVE
The Golden Era

The telephone systems for the summer school programs were not functioning yet, and cell phones were not that popular back then. She said she would be there studying for the Maryland Educational Certification exam all weekend.

I examined the information she had written on the napkin. From her neat big, bubbled, cursive penmanship, I noted that we resided in the same Argonne Apartments.

"You know you stay in the same apartment complex as I do but on the opposite side, on the third floor?"

"So, it shouldn't be too difficult to find me."

She flirtatiously responded.

Feeling like I had accomplished something significant or closed the deal, I politely thanked Redbone for the stimulating conversation and looked forward to seeing her again. I returned to where Fifty Grand and I initially sat in the busy cafeteria.

Fifty was hunched over his plate like a hungry, protective junkyard dog. He asked in his heavy, nerdish Bronx accent.

"Yo, what's good with you and Mello Yellow?"

HISTORICALLY BLACK LOVE
The Golden Era

"From my observation, I sensed good molecular chemistry. You two were clicking and seemed to enjoy each other's company and dialogue?"

He added in a slurred voice.

"She seems cool and is from outside of Chicago,"

I said casually.

." She hit me off with her information and invited me to stop by her spot later. She said she would be studying for some educational exam."

As I curiously glanced at the information she'd transcribed on the napkin.

At that time, I wasn't quite sure about my intentions with her. Chi-Town didn't come off as phony or disingenuous, but I had reservations that she would be studying for a test on a summer Friday night. There were always get-togethers and parties on campus, especially in Charm City. I was somewhat skeptical. Morgan State University is a renowned party school, and I did not know anyone who didn't get their party on at the offset of the weekend. Besides, who studies on a Friday?

14 Vibes and Stuff

Fifty Grand and I finished our meals and vacated the refractory. We decided to stroll across campus and check out the university's landscape.

As we exited the rear of the building, the weekend's vibe greeted us with gleeful enthusiasm. Young scholars mingled on the patio in the middle of the dormitories of the all-male New Building, the all-female Blount Towers, and the co-ed Argonne Apartments. After a long enduring week of hitting the books, it was a day party and a swell way to jump-start the weekend.

The summer semester was noticeably more relaxed and less dense with students, and the campus was less hyper and manic than during the fall and spring semesters. The academic and social burdens were not as intense during the summer, so the pressure to front, impress, and act like we were coping was significantly reduced. Regardless of the semester, the campus always got crunk on the weekends.

As we began to trek across campus with no destination in mind, the buzz of the start of the weekend could be felt by the music thumping in the background.

The eclectic sounds of music played an essential role in Black college life. Remember how I told you that Hip-Hop was my first love before I met Redbone? Well, Morgan State did its part to contribute and cultivate that relationship.

HISTORICALLY BLACK LOVE
The Golden Era

From every sector of the university, some form of music consumed the environment. The rhythmic, hyper-pulsating sounds of B-More's house music, the distinctive, heavy sounds of the bass and drums of D.C.'s Go-Go, and hypnotic Hip-Hop reverberated throughout the atmosphere of the historically Black college campus constantly, and especially on the weekends.

During homecoming celebration week and the Grand Homecoming Step Show, the biggest Hip-Hop acts, groups such as Biggie Smalls and the Junior Mafia, Wu-Tang Clan, Meth and Redman, Naughty by Nature, Nas, and the likes—all performed in Morgan's Hill Field House.

I had the privileged to witness the Fugees, Lauryn Hill, and Maxwell tear it down in the Murphy Auditorium during the 'ninety-four Homecoming, just before they all blew up into genuine international superstars.

Morgan's Student Government Association often sponsored events and invited Hip-Hop artists and industry insiders to the Mckeldin Center to discuss the many dynamics of the music and entertainment industries. The Neo-Soul R&B group *Groove Theory* came to the McKeldin Center and spoke with the students about the ends and outs of the music industry.

In Dr. Stevenson's Speech class, I performed a rendition of Common Sense's, now known as Common, classic Hip-Hop anthem, *"I Used to Love H.E.R."* The first single off his classic sophomore album Resurrection.

HISTORICALLY BLACK LOVE
The Golden Era

The classic anthem is about a young man's expression of love, respect, and passion for the genre of Hip-Hop and its evolution in the music industry over the last few decades. Common personifies Hip-Hop as a female he falls deeply in love with and expresses how he came to depend on her in every aspect of his life. The poet also articulates how he endures and tolerates her indecisions and the difficulties of being in the music industry. I was able to bring the poem to life and sell it, as I was instructed by Dr. Stevenson, using hand, facial expressions, and gestures.

In a stanza of the poem, Common expresses he was" *sitting on the bone, wishing he could do her,"* meaning having the ability and skills to spit beautiful, poetic rhymes. In front of the entire class, I clutched my gonads, closed my eyes, and passionately recited that bar as if wishing or praying that I could make love to her or have the ability to spit poetic rhymes at the drop of a dime.

I received a rousing standing ovation from my classmates for my standout performance. I earned my first A+ letter grade as a Morgan student. Dr. Stevenson wrote on my evaluation form, "Excellent! My confidence expanded significantly from that experience.

The university received love from the Hip-Hop community and was an essential epicenter for disseminating the culture along the Mid-Atlantic.

Morgan was equipped with one of the most popular college Hip-Hop radio shows on the East coast, *Strictly Hip-Hop,* on the school's Smooth Jazz station, 89.9, WEAA. On the weekends, S*trictly* played all the latest Hip-Hop classics and broke new artists' records regularly.

Each weekend Hip-Hop artists and groups would frequent the radio station and give insightful interviews about their projects, careers, and the ins and outs of the music industry. When I became a Communications major, I learned how to cipher off some of those Hip-Hop artists, leaving their *Strictly* interviews and conducting my own.

I would patiently wait outside the radio station studio after the radio host interviewed them. I graciously introduced myself, invited them downstairs to the television studios in the Banneker Building, and conducted my interviews, which I submitted as class assignments.

Many of the interviews would be produced in the wee hours of the morning. Keith Murry of the Def Squad, the wordsmith, is a bugged-out but entertaining emcee and person.

The Wu-Tang Clan shouted out Morgan State on their first single, *Protect Yak Neck,* off their classic debut album, *36 Chambers,* certifying Morgan as a Hip-Hop institution.

Joe Claire, a 93 Morgan graduate and the host of the iconic hit music video program on Black Entertainment Television, B.E.T.'s *Rap City*, kept Morgan on the Hip-Hop map. Claire shouted out to Morgan regularly on Rap City and produced several episodes of the show from Morgan's campus.

HISTORICALLY BLACK LOVE
The Golden Era

The dime-piece, Tisha Campbell, co-star of the smash hit sitcom *Martin*, often sported blue and orange Morgan State gear, sweatshirts, and hoodies in many of the iconic sitcom's episodes. Morgan State significantly represented HBCUs and Hip-Hop culture during the Golden Era in the mid-nineties.

Whether in the dorms, refractory, or anywhere on campus, you could stumble upon an open mic, poetry slam, or emcees huddled up in a cipher, spitting colorful freestyle rhymes. Sundays were tranquil with the traditional gospel and classic sounds of R&B greats like Frankie Beverly & Maze, Bob Marley, Prince, and the likes hovering in the air.

During the summer of 95, Notorious B I G's debut, the critically acclaimed, *Ready to Die,* was easily the most consumed album on campus. Every stereo in every dorm room and vehicles driving by seemed to be rocking one of the banging tracks off the CD.

Ready To Die was the official soundtrack of the summer, and "Juicy" will forever be one of Hip-Hop's greatest anthems. Christopher Wallace was a grandmaster on the microphone and catapulted lyricism to an utterly new stratification. His flow, breath control, and vivid details of the pictures he painted were incredible. The witty and intelligent wordplay, metaphors, double-entendres, and the emotions his lyrics invoked—no other Hip-Hop artist did it better.

As O.J. and I strolled across the campus, the sounds of Big's music meshed with the landscape of the Baltimore historically Black university, setting the tone for the weekend.

HISTORICALLY BLACK LOVE
The Golden Era

We strolled across Morgan's majestic campus to the vibes of the luscious grounds saturated with beautiful young ladies on that tranquil Friday summer evening. We mixed and mingled with folks we knew and flirted with several girls along the way. We eventually crossed the Welcome Bridge and entered the North campus, where many academic and administration buildings were neatly nuzzled.

The heartbeat and social center of the school were the Mckeldin Student Center; it was always activity in the building, Student Government Association functions, conferences, lectures from guest speakers, fund-raisers, and political campaigns. Mckeldin was also a comfortable space to lounge, chill, and socialize.

The Carter-Grant Administration Building, Truth Hall, the Lois T. Murphy Education Center, Callaway, and Carnegie Halls were all neatly situated in the quad. The Banneker Communications Building was also located in the yard and the academic hall where I would spend most of my time as a Media Communications major, learning the Magic of directing, producing, and editing.

With the majestic bronze statue of Fredrick Douglas stationed in the front of the building, Holmes Hall was the centerpiece of the North Campus. Next to Holmes Hall was the Harriett Tubman House, an all-freshman female honor's dormitory. Young men were always sniffing around the building, trying to expose and exploit any possible opportunities. The dorm was locked down like Fort Knox; it seemed like you needed to have government credentials just to step foot in the building.

HISTORICALLY BLACK LOVE
The Golden Era

Within the confines of these modern structures of the campus, there were plenty of spaces full of beautiful, healthy green grass. It was explained to us by a renowned professor who'd once attended Morgan in the mid-seventies that the famed North campus green spaces were a completely different scene and vibe.

The professor painted a picture of how it was back in those days. He said the green spaces were filled with students rocking big afros, wearing colorful dashikis, stretched out on blankets, listening to Stevie Wonder, soaking up the Sun, and inhaling plenty of cannabis smoke. He said the green spaces were like a mini-Woodstock and claimed a considerable marijuana cloud loomed over the North campus daily around noon.

During the *Golden Era,* my generation of Morganites, we'd smoked plenty of weed, but we couldn't fathom laying on the grass, listening to Outkast's *Southernplayalisticadillacmuzik* smoking blunts. We were too sophisticated and couldn't afford to get our Polo's dirty and our Timbs scuffed up.

As we traveled across the Bridge in front of the Soper Library, we ran into the *D.C. Duo,* Mack, and *Cool-Ass Dre.* They were always together and held from Southeast D.C. They both were Business majors. Morgan, at that time, had one of the most esteemed business programs among all HBCUs.

Dre and Mack represented D.C., Go-Go culture to the fullest. They always rocked double extra-large, all-black or grey sweatpants and t-shirts, crispy grey New Balance sneakers, or Timbs with the thick-ass double-layered tubes socks. Their baseball cap brims were bent towards the sky, and Mack always sported the classic Hip-Hop Gazelle sunglasses.

We politicked with the Duo for a few minutes, anticipating the clash of the N.B.A. Finals that was about to start in a few. I invited them to fall through our spot a little later to watch the game and throw something up in the air. We gave them each a pound and kept stepping across campus.

Parallel to Morgan's basketball arena, the Hill Field House. Morgan's Magnificent Marching Machine, the school's marching band, was assembled across the Bears' practice football field. They were rehearsing a spirited rendition of the beloved, classic anthem of Frankie Beverly and Maze's *"Before I Let You Go.*

A culture jewel we cherish and associate with the best times and memories of being around loved ones, friends, and family. *Before I Let You Go* is played at all cookouts and family celebrations, it will get the party popping and the Soul Train line rocking. It's not considered a family reunion without Frankie Beverly and Maze playing in the background while someone passes a large dish of tangy potato salad. The passion and expression of love in Frankie's voice, timeless guitar riff, and melody take you away to another time and place. The song touches the souls of Black folks.

One of the most extraordinary sensations I've ever experienced at Morgan was singing, *Before I Let You Go,* during the 94 Homecoming football game. Singin in unison with a stadium full of beautiful Black people. It was a super standout proud moment as a student at Morgan.

HISTORICALLY BLACK LOVE
The Golden Era

Before I Let You Go, the song transcends time and space and is loved by all generations of Black folks. The young and seasoned, swaying back and forth with a smooth two-step, hands in the atmosphere, clapping to the beat, was so great, and a unique vibe and a moment burned into my soul. I fell in love with my Black people; I felt privileged, proud, and honored to be a part of such a grand spectacle.

We maintained and watched Morgan's Marching Machine for a few minutes, absorbing the good vibes flowing from the horns and thunderous drumline. Watching the band members move as a unit as they gyrated and coordinated with style and precision entertained and lifted our spirits at that moment, along with a few other spectators.

During the Golden Era, we die heart Morganites would primarily attend the football games just to watch the Morgan Marching Machine and the Battle of the Bands and be entertained by the Drum Major. It was also an enjoyable time to cut loose and get your dance on rather than watch the dismal performance of the Bears' weak football team.

In the mid-nineties, Morgan's football team was nothing to brag about and light-years away from the legendary days of Coach "Eddied P" Hurt's teams, winning fourteen CIAA and six Black College Championships and sustained the longest college football winning streak of thirty-one wins in the mid-sixties.

The Battle of the Bands at halftime at historically Black colleges and universities football and basketball games was sometimes more anticipated than the sporting event itself. You were apprehensive about going to the restroom or getting a snack because the shows were just that exciting and entertaining. You didn't want to miss a second of the halftime show.

The rich music the bands recited was directly tethered to our culture, traditions, and history of great musical GOATs such as Michael Jackson, Aretha Franklyn, James Brown, Marvin Gaye, and many others. I never felt the music from bands from PWIs the way I did at Morgan or other Black schools.

The rhythms and beats from the Magnificent Marching Machine were more familiar. They massaged my spirits, perpetuating a profound sense of pride. HBCU bands were flamboyant and flashy and came with many styles that set things off and got the crowd excited and ready to celebrate.

As we weaved between the Argonne Apartments to get to our suite, we encountered Tisha from Las Vegas and her crew of sores. Tish was a proud, die-hard AKA and always represented her sorority at every opportunity. If it was pink and green in one form or another, Tish was non-stop, twenty-four-seven with it. Be it shoes, sneakers, sweatshirts or pants, t-shirts, head wraps, pens or buttons, bed sheets, pillowcases, panties, bras, bathrobes, and toothbrushes. If the Morgan Book Store has something with the AKA letters and symbols or was pink and green, bets believe Tish copped it.

No matter how hard I tried, Tish refused to reveal any secrets or activities she had to undertake to become a part of the exclusive

HISTORICALLY BLACK LOVE
The Golden Era

AKA sisterhood. Shit, the topic wasn't even up for discussion, period!

Tish and I were cool; she was one of the initial females at Morgan to befriend me. I took a liking to Tish because she was an authentic Hip Hopper. She had stacks of Hip-Hop CDs. We often stayed up late until the a.m. listening to music. She put me on too many West-Coast artists and musicians, such as E-40, Mac-Dre, and the Souls of Mischief.

She sometimes cooked for our crew if we provided the necessary groceries. She was a culinary goddess in the kitchen and prepared the juiciest, crispiest fried chicken my mouth has ever tasted.

We kicked it with Tish and her crew for a few. She threw me some rhythm with her big bright smile and flirtatious eye contact and invited Fifty and me back to their spot to get down with a Spades tournament. I told her,

"I'll see."

I wasn't quite sure what my plans consisted of for that evening. I was still intrigued by the stimulating conversation I had with Redbone earlier in the refractory.

We returned to our complex and jogged up the stairs to get to our suite. Many immature souls, along with the electricity of living in the moment, with the Friday night shenanigans, loomed over the Black college campus; you could feel it; it was thick.

118

15 Party Suite

As we entered our suite, a strong aroma of chronic and the funky sounds of Snoop Dogg & Tha Dog Pound's, It Ain't No Fun greeted our noses and ears. We had one of the numerous party suites on campus. From Thursday to early Sunday morning, it was a continuous animal house, a non-stop party; it was on and popping in our layer. It was always a reason for a celebration in our suite.

The atmosphere was like the Barnum and Baily circus. Hip Hop was blasting out of the stereo. Females of all types were scattered throughout the suite; some I'd recognized and other randoms I didn't. They seemed to be doing cartwheels, summersaults, and back handsprings down the hallway running in and out of every room.

My man LB, a bright-yellow bi-racial dude from Sacramento, was sitting at the dining table with his Cali compadres crumbling and twisting up good herb. They were working with at least a half-ounce.

Another clan of loud, rumbustious guys, about twelve to fifteen, were clustered on the couch and chairs around a 36-inch Zenith television, all sipping on red cups or gripping Heineken bottles or both.

Game one of the 95' NBA Finals was about to commence. The defending champions, the Houston Rockets, Hakeem the *Dream*, and the *Jet* Kenny Smith, were battling the Orlando Magic and a

119

young, brash Shaquille O'Neil and Penny Hardaway for the coveted hardware of an NBA World Championship ring. Michael Jordan retired to pursue a career in professional baseball two years earlier.

The frizzy was up with the game on; the suite was lit, and everything was full blast. I tried to chill, engage, and watch the first half of the game with the fellas but couldn't get into the basketball contest and the surrounding festivities.

I hadn't consumed a drop of alcohol, and when one of the many blunts in the rotation was passed off to me, I uncharacteristically declined. Redbone from the Mid-West and our conversation was still dangling heavily in my mind. Her voice, our dialog and vibe superseded all the activities around me.

I was perplexed. Before this day, I had never seen this female on Morgan's campus; I'm sure I would have remembered her baby doll face. Why hadn't I seen her around? I thought I knew most folks on campus and desired to learn more about her.

I wasn't sure what my intentions were with this girl I had just met. The situation felt different and vital. She was unlike any other female I encountered at Morgan. She made a compelling, mysterious first impression on me. Her energy was unique and sexy. I had to investigate and learn more about her before the opportunity vanished. I abruptly jumped off the couch, gave all the fellas watching the basketball game some dap, and was out.

"Coli Coles, where are you going? It's only first-half?" asked Fifty Grand.

HISTORICALLY BLACK LOVE
The Golden Era

"I'm going to check the Redbone, Mello Yellow, the shorty from the Mid-West I met in the refractory earlier at dinner."

I'm sure if Michael Jordan were playing in the Finals, I would have stayed and watched the entire contest. I was a huge Michael Jordan fan, but since he wasn't playing in the championship, Redbone it was.

"Good luck, homie!" OJ shouted.

I washed up and put on a clean pair of underwear and a fresh, black Polo. I brushed my teeth and inserted my contacts, grabbed the Yankee fitted and a couple of Magnums out of the top drawer of my desk, and bounced focused.

16 Focused!

Under normal circumstances, I would have taken my time and let things marinate for a few days or so before I attempted to hook up with a potential new friend. However, it was something special about this one. Based on our short conversation in the refractory, I had this prevailing feeling she was different. I wanted to explore and better understand this sense of urgency I was experiencing.

Redbone resided in the Argonne Complex on the opposite side on the third floor. I was nervous yet focused as I anxiously ascended the three flights of stairs to get to her suite. As I stood on the third-floor patio, I glanced across the campus and noticed the sun glimmering with a pinkish metallic glow. It dangled magically low in the grey Baltimore sky. The air was cool and breezy.

I took a deep breath and knocked on the aluminum door. A tall, attractive, mocha-brown-skinned female with long micro braids sporting a bright orange Morgan State hoodie, black Nike spandex, and long-eared pink bunny slippers answered the door.

The female who answered the door looked familiar; I recognized her as a women's volleyball team member. Although I never knew her name, we'd acknowledged each other with a simple hello or what's up on campus? She graciously allowed me to enter the common area of the suite. We exchanged a few words of pleasantries about being in summer school.

HISTORICALLY BLACK LOVE
The Golden Era

My first impression of their spot was a clean, well-organized, comfortable space. The natural aroma of a fresh bouquet of colorful flowers on the coffee table consumed the room, and it instantly put me at ease and was quite relaxing compared to my spot on the other side of the building.

My suite was always congested with big, sweaty, testosterone-driven athletes, loud Hip-Hop or Go-Go blasting music, mad chicken heads, and plenty of chicken wings. Our spot was infinitely saturated with constant drama. Their suite had a wholesome, clean academic vibe—a place where you could concentrate and get your academics on.

I explained to Bunny Slippers, who I was here to see. In an attempt to pronounce her name, I butchered it up. Luckily, she understood who I was referencing and directed me where I needed to go.

"The second room on the left."

I politely thanked her for the assistance and proceeded down the atrium, still focused.

17 Wow!

As I approached her room, I wasn't sure what to expect. I met this female a couple of hours ago; I kept my mind and expectations open to all possibilities. If the vibe ain't right, then I am leaving.

She could be a psycho-chic struggling with mental issues. She could be a straight-up freak who knows what she likes and wants; a jump-off could pop off. Or she could be a weirdo, dirty, nasty, or contaminated in some way; you never know with females. I was hoping for the best but prepared for the worst.

Her door was slightly cracked open; I tapped it with one of my keys. In her signature, Mid-Western twang, she said,

"Come in."

I pushed open the door to a reasonably neat and clean room. Redbone was perched up on one of the twin beds with her legs crossed in an Indian fashion. She was pleasantly surprised to see me and greeted me with a warm, bright smile.

"Hey, you, Chicken Man Dan!" she giggled.

"Oh, you got jokes. I was in your neck of the woods and thought I'd stop by and say hi. I hope I didn't disrupt this academic situation?".

HISTORICALLY BLACK LOVE
The Golden Era

"No, you didn't. It's perfect timing; I'm glad you stopped by. I could use a break from all this studying; my brain hurts."

She looked even more impressive than I remembered from earlier at dinner. In my head, I thought, *Wow! She is more beautiful than I remember.*

To my surprise, she had all these books and papers scattered across her bed while the other divan was covered with books and articles. She was pursuing a bachelor's in Education and was studying for a state exam on a Friday night.

I initially saw this young lady as a nerd with a sense of humor. I was impressed; it's something super sexy and impressive about an intelligent and attractive woman. She was a Tender Roni.

Redbone brushed aside some books and papers and graciously invited me to sit next to her. I was even more pleased to learn she was an all-natural—not a drop of make-up, no weaves, not even a glimmer of lip gloss. Redbone was nothing but pure unadulterated beauty.

She wasn't wearing anything fancy, just some faded Levi jeans and a graphic t-shirt. She smelled like a fresh shower and a hint of baby powder. A thin, gold necklace complemented by a tiny crucifix dangled from her neck and adorned her porcelain smooth, caramel skin.

HISTORICALLY BLACK LOVE
The Golden Era

She was not wearing any socks and had pretty feet. They were small with high arches and clean, pedicured toes. Her hair was thick, healthy, coffee brown, and hung to her shoulders. It was pulled back into a simple ponytail, with a sky blue scrounge wrapped around it. Thin Shirley Temple curls drooped down across her baby doll face. She'd swiped the dangling lock to the side and wrapped it around the back of her left ear so as not to impede direct eye contact. I was relaxed, looking directly into her soul, inviting brown eyes.

She had beautiful sexy, manicured hands and fingers without jewelry or fingernail polish. Natural French tips, filed at slight angles to top it off. Her nose was round and proportional to her flawless face. Cute, chubby, chipmunk cheeks cradled her full luscious lips, pearl white bright teeth, and impeccable smile. Her beauty was simply magnetic.

I sensed Redbone might be going through a few personal issues. Her energy felt melancholy; something seemed to be weighing on her heavily. I was picking up on heartbreak, loneliness, or homesickness. Whatever personal dilemmas or struggles she was coping with then, I also perceived she needed worthy company and a good laugh.

18 Loungin'

Janet Jackson's *Janet* CD softly played in the background, setting the mood for a relaxing casual situation. Instantly I felt at home and comfortable being around her and in her space alone.

I felt like I could kick off my Jordans and stretch out across her bed like we were homies. I had to remind myself I had just met this female only a few hours ago. I remained disciplined and kept my Js on.

We lounged for the next four hours, listening to the sounds of Mary J. Blige, Usher, Xscape, TLC, and a few other artists. She had no Hip-Hop amongst the stack of CDs, only R&B and a few gospel joints such as Yolanda Adams, Bee Bee, Cee Cee, and Sounds of Blackness.

We conversed about what seemed like everything under the sun, getting acquainted with one another. Our initial conversation was a continuation of dinner but more in-depth about where we were from. She represented the Midwest and a suburb just north of Chicago; I was reppin' New England— Springfield, Massachusetts, to be exact.

"You're kidding. You've never heard of Springfield, Massachusetts. The birthplace of basketball, the greatest spectator sport on Earth, invented by Dr. James Naismith back in 1891 at Springfield College?"

I gasped and was confused because I thought that information was common knowledge. She shrugged her shoulders, looking dumbfounded.

"I have heard of Springfield, *Illinois*,"

she stated.

"It's the capital and the birthplace of the United States' sixteenth President, Abraham Lincoln. Isn't the popular cartoon *The Simpsons* based in Springfield?"

She sarcastically asked with a sinister chuckle.

"You know the Snoop D O Double G video "*Gin n' Juice*"? The blue and green hockey jersey he is wearing is my city's minor *American Hockey League* team, the one with the large Native American head and the S on the chest. The Springfield Indians of Springfield, Massachusetts,

I said proudly.

"Also, the great Dr. Seuss is from the Field, Smith & Wesson, the Webster's Dictionary, the first automobile, and radio station are all from my hometown, *"The City of First,"* Springfield, Massachusetts, you better recognize.

HISTORICALLY BLACK LOVE
The Golden Era

We both laughed in concert; it was a good first lap around the track, set the tone and pace for the remainder of the evening, and helped us get acquainted with one another.

We switched lanes and began to discuss living in Baltimore and our observations and understanding of the city. We compared the music, people, and cultures from our perspectives.

Charm City was much different than we both expected and imagined. It was much larger geographically —it was at least ten times larger than Springfield. I'd anticipated Baltimore would be more progressive; its kinetic energy was notably slower than the Northeast.

Chicago played a more significant social, economic, and cultural impact on the region, country, and globe, which we discussed in detail. She described Chicago's efficient transportation system as far superior to B-More's.

She mentioned how she and her sisters would often take adventurous excursions into Chi City by catching the train and spending all day hunting for bargains, shoes, and other original garments. I sensed she missed Chicago's cosmopolitan hustle and bustle.

Baltimore was a blue-collar town, and most of its residents were African Americans. It was also saturated with pockets of poverty, narcotics, crime, and violence. The public education system was on life support, about to collapse in on itself. Back in the mid-ninnies, the whole city could use a stimulus plan. In some places, it just wasn't safe.

One afternoon, on a solo sightseeing escapade, I inconspicuously stumbled into the wrong neighborhood in West Baltimore. The vibe and sky suddenly transformed from bright and sunny to dark and gloomy. It felt like I was suddenly on the set of Michael Jackson's *"Thriller"* video; no exaggeration, shit got real, really quick.

The environment transformed into hostile territory; trash and debris were scattered everywhere. The roll houses were all worn down and dilapidated. Hustlers, goons, and goblins seemed to be perched upon the porches, hanging out of the windows and in the streets.

I begin to feel very uncomfortable; my Spidey senses start to tingle. I felt like prey to the natives, the way they were curiously gazing upon me. I didn't fit in; It was obvious I was an out-of-towner. I sensed them sizing me up, wondering who I was and why I was strolling through their hood. It was a bad look; I made a quick U-turn and retreated to safer, more familiar grounds.

As students at Morgan, Redbone and I were exposed and emerged in the Go-Go music scene. The whole thing was strange to an actual Hip-Hop head. The amount of Go-Go we were subjected to while down in Baltimore was extensive, and it took some time to adapt and adjust to the foreign-sounding music.

My roommates from D.C. were torturing me with the heavy percussion-sounding music. Twenty-four hours, seven days a week, they would crank up Chuck Brown, Rare Essence, or the Backyard

HISTORICALLY BLACK LOVE
The Golden Era

Band to excessive volumes and rock out. They weren't fucking with anything Hip Hop. No EPMD, Redman, Keith Murray, Snoop, Dr. Dre, Outkast, or Wu-Tang Clan. Just Go-Go music all day and night long. Back then, I was wrong when I thought everybody listened to some Hip-Hop, not these D.C. dudes; it was strictly Go-Go.

The only Go-Go I was exposed to before becoming a student in Baltimore was the classic single, the *Da Butt,* by Experience Unlimited. That was a definitive party jam.

Da But was the first song that inspired me to take a real chance on the dance floor. I got up on a girl for the first time doing *Da But* at the Berkeley Ballroom, a Hip-Hop Friday night spot for teenagers in the Field. Besides that, one classic song, I knew nothing about Go-Go music and was completely ignorant about its culture.

I was invited to accompany my roommate and a couple of his homies to an actual live Go-Go in Southeast D.C. That was one of the most bizarre experiences of my life. I gained a greater appreciation and understanding of Go-Go music and its rich D.C. culture; it was authentic and original. Go-Go had its own texture, feel, and vibe.

A Go-Go is a D.C. cultural party or event equipped with a band centered around the percussions and bass. The term Go-Go refers to the party that will continue to go on and on until the break of dawn; thus, the term Go-Go describes the event.

HISTORICALLY BLACK LOVE
The Golden Era

The best way I can describe my experience at my first Go-Go was being directly connected to my ancestors from the motherland. There was a spiritual presence in the building, something I'd never experienced before at a party. The heavy, pounding beats and rhythms were exotic and intoxicating and teleported me back to the African continent.

The Go-Go band and DJ entertained the partygoers for most of the evening. The band would play a few sets, and then the DJ would spin the latest Hip-Hop and R&B joints; the vibe was right and balanced. The party's momentum gradually picked up pace throughout the evening. Then suddenly, with the heavy crank of the percussions, everyone seemed to be summoned to the middle of the dance floor. The energy and vibe of the party completely shifted with the quickness.

The partygoers coordinated with the band's heavy sounds; they began to create a large circle in the middle of the dance floor. The females danced in the center while the males surrounded them in this rhythmic dance, and everybody chanted. The percussion was so thick and heavy that they put you in a hazy intoxicating trance.

It was like an African tribal ritual dance taking place right before me. Some females were so caught up in a rapture they began to take their shirts off and rub on their titties; it was bugged and too much for me. You had to grow up in the culture to appreciate the music and their customs entirely—at least, that was how it was explained to me.

"If you're from the Northeast, there is only so much Chuck, Junk Yard, and House you can tolerate," I'd confessed.

HISTORICALLY BLACK LOVE
The Golden Era

Being from the Chicago area, Redbone was familiar with the huge House music scene and how heavy it was in B-More and the vast underground scene in the Chi but wasn't a big fan of the genre. She was strictly an R&B and gospel girl.

I went to a couple of House music clubs in B-More; it felt like I was in the Thunder Dome movie. The music was loud and impulsive, and the way the partygoers danced to the music was just as wild and impulsive as the House music being played. It was cool and different, but it wasn't my cup of tea. I couldn't get into the music, and the homosexual crowd was represented heavily in the building.

We both agreed that the folks from the Northeast had attitudes and walked around with a chip on their shoulders or like they were entitled. Northeasterners were more hostile, easily offended, and antagonistic compared to people from other parts of the country and the world for that matter.

She ranted, "You can't even say hi to some people from the North without them catching an attitude."

Redbone mentioned how a few Brooklyn females got out of pocket with her. She had to redirect and check them quickly to let them know she wasn't the one.

We appreciated Charm City's unique culture of seafood, crab cakes, and the world-famous Baltimore Harbor. Townson Mall was also an excellent way to escape campus life, which many Morganites took advantage of by catching the shuttle bus to the mall provided by Morgan.

We shared some of our high school highlights and experiences. Redbone received several academic accolades and scholastic honors and was the first African American to address the graduating class at her high school.

I mentioned my high school athletic experiences and achievements, such as MVP on the football team and receiving the Coach's Awards playing basketball, and my short stint on Morgan's basketball team as a walk-on.

As a member of Morgan's Men's basketball team for a brief period, I was blessed with an opportunity to receive an education beyond the classroom.

After a game against Ole Miss on ESPN, Coach chartered a bus from Oxford, Mississippi, to Memphis, Tennessee, to the Motel-Lorraine, where Dr. Martin Luther King Jr. was slain on April 4, 1968. The motel was converted into a Civil Rights Museum. The Civil Rights gallery provided a powerful insight into the Civil Rights movement and the struggle we as a people are still fighting. The field trip made a lasting impression on the entire team.

Our conversation revealed that we were the third child of four, just the opposite gender. I had two older brothers and a baby sister, and she had two older sisters and a baby brother. We compared the advantages and disadvantages of being the middle child.

HISTORICALLY BLACK LOVE
The Golden Era

"Man, it sure was rough growing up in a family as the middle child," she said emotionally.

"I never got to go shopping like my two older sisters. They would come home with all these shopping bags, the latest fashions, the cutesiest outfits, and nothing for me. They would pass down old clothes they didn't want any more or were out of style. I barely got anything new until I got older and could fend for myself. I always got their hand-me-downs!"

The experience seemed to have traumatized her to some degree.

Empathizing with her ordeal, I said, "Sometimes I would sneak into my brother's closet and wear one of their shirts to school and deal with the consequences when I got home."

She agreed that was also one of her motes of operation, wearing her sister's clothes without permission. We both got a good chuckle from that notion.

We also agreed it seemed as though we always got the brunt of the blame for the trouble that went down in our households. The baby of the bunch— my sister and her brother—were too cute and precious to get beat or punished. Meanwhile, our two older siblings always stuck together as a team and learned how to maneuver their way out of tight situations.

HISTORICALLY BLACK LOVE
The Golden Era

"I swear my baby brother never got any spankings or beat in the manner I did," she groaned.

"He could get caught with his hand in the cookie jar and get off scot-free!"

"I only witnessed my sister get beat once; I loved every bit of the three weak swats my mother assaulted her with," I revealed.

We both thought it was our primary responsibility to protect our youngest sibling at all costs.

"Anybody touched my brother; they had to deal with me growing up!" she declared. I was the same too.

"My father assigned me as my baby sister's protector, and I took my job seriously," I said proudly,

"If you messed with my sister, you had to deal with me."

I earned my very first knockout under my belt when I was sixteen. This big Black greasy dude kept bullying my sister. Whenever she came out onto the block, he would say intimidating things that made her uncomfortable and concerned, such as she was his girlfriend and that she had better show him respect whenever he was around.

HISTORICALLY BLACK LOVE
The Golden Era

"My sister would come home disturbed, crying, and shaken. I searched for the dude for two weeks, and when I finally tracked him down, my crew and I escorted him back to my block. I instructed my man Ralphie to go up the backstairs and tell my sister to come onto the front porch to identify him. When she confirmed it was him, it was lights out! He hit the concrete trembling and convulsing. Blood was gushing out of his mouth and nose after I hit him with a forceful two-piece. From then on, nobody on the block ever messed with my baby sister again."

Redbone grew quiet for a moment. She was a little disturbed by the violence but understood it was my baby sister I was protecting.

As she reached across my body, touching my shoulder and arm to help support herself. I noticed how her touch made me feel; it was a strange sensation; it felt right. I craved more of her touch.

She picked up a small brown leather photo album and showed me several pictures of her and her family, identifying each sibling, their age, and something particular about them. The photo reminded me of the hit sitcom in the mid-nineties, the Bill Cosby Show's Huxtable family. They gave an impression of a loving, dignified household, and I sensed the pride, love, and loyalty she possessed for her clan.

Redbone said she attended Morgan after her parents hosted her on a personal HBCU tour. Her family drove across the South, visiting other historically Black institutions like Tuskegee, Southern, Grambling, and several others. She explained how Morgan left the best impression on her among all the colleges they visited. She liked the programs they offered at Morgan, the campus was beautiful, and the facilities were modern.

We both thought there was something special about Morgan State University and how the school complemented our styles. The university was progressive and possessed the traditional Black institution vibe. We'd also agreed that Morgan's Welcome Bridge sealed the deal.

Our conversation continued to switch gears and seamlessly discussed the many dynamics of the "*Black College Experience* " and the successes and challenges we'd encountered as students at Morgan.

Getting acclimated to an all-Black academic environment was a challenge for us on many levels. We both seriously considered transferring to another institution at one time or another. Being in an environment surrounded by all-Black folks can be challenging on many levels and can force you to find beauty and strength in yourself and your people. We'd endured and wouldn't exchange our "*Black College Experience*" for anything else.

We derived a keen sense of personal pride and unique honor from attending a historically Black university. It was precisely where we wanted to be.

The collective consciousness, the critical responsibility to our people and race, and the acknowledgment of our ancestor's struggles and great history could best be obtained and preserved by attending a historically Black college. It allows us to search for the best in ourselves and provide a solid foundation to explore Black excellence.

That was important to both of us—to be a part of the legacy of African American scholars, visionaries, and leaders. Redbone had a sincere sense of purpose and wanted to represent our people without compromise. I thought that quality in her was so sexy. I also developed that same sense of purpose while working at Martin Luther King. Jr. Community Center as a Youth Coordinator before I went to school down in B-more.

We began to explore the many dynamics of attending a Black school; our conversation swerved onto the topic of pledging. Redbone stated that if she did choose to pledge, it would be red and white of the Delta Sigma Theta Sorority. If she did, she would have fit right in. The Deltas, to me, were the finest on campus. They were intelligent, graceful, and sophisticated, second to none. The Delta's were on a Michelle Obama or Beyoncé quality level.

If I had decided to pledge, it would have been the purple and gold of the Omega Psi Phi Fraternity. Not only did the Q-Dogs have a confident swagger I could appreciate and relate to, but the Qs also had mad pull, swag, and respect on campus and got things done. They encompassed a sense of loyalty and strength that resonated within me. I also admired the gold spray-painted Timberland boots they rocked on campus. At that time, we were both indecisive about when and if we would pledge.

The conversation continued to flow into our future goals, aspirations, and dreams. Redbone said that her goal was to earn her

Ph.D. in Education. I stated that I was undeclared, but I would be the best at whatever I decided.

Throughout our conversation, we learned that we had many things in common. We also discovered that we were from entirely different worlds, opposites.

Our situation was like the Bill Cosby Show's spin-off, *It's A Different World,* the situational comedy about young college students and their "Black College Experience" at the fictional Hillman College. Redbone and I were from different worlds, attending the real Morgan State University.

Being an Army Brat, I was privileged to be exposed to many diverse types of people, cultures, and the world. In my pre-teens, I lived in Texas, Kentucky, overseas in Germany, then back to my birthplace of Springfield, Massachusetts.

I was raised in the hood and developed certain instincts to help me survive and advance. I did my best to articulate to Redbone that I was a survivor, who I was, and my current situation. I didn't front; I kept it as honest as I could. I was a good man with a good heart and would find my way.

I was on my own; I had no dedicated parents to call in my times of need. I wasn't receiving care packages with toiletries, new socks, underwear, t-shirts, and home-cooked meals. I was registered as an independent student; I made all my choices and decisions on my own and depended on student loans, grants, and scholarships to pay my way through school.

HISTORICALLY BLACK LOVE
The Golden Era

Redbone was a refined, privileged, and cultured young lady. She was raised in a stable household and lived in a suburb in the same home her entire life. She never settled or struggled for anything; all her needs were satisfied. She was insulated from many of life's ills because her parents were college-educated professionals who nurtured and supported all her endeavors. Redbone expressed that she was raised in the church, and her faith was vital to her.

With all our differences, strangely, we complemented one another. We balanced each other; my weaknesses were her strengths, and vice versa. My strength and her beauty were the perfect combination.

19 Temptations

During our stimulating conversation, I will admit I was oscillating in my mind, going back and forth, debating if I should try to smash it or not.

I tried to rationalize. What other reason am I here for? It's Friday night. I just hooked up with this fine female, we are all alone, and I got a pocket full of condoms. The math was quite simple, smash and dash. In any other situation, it would have been as simple as that. But this *wasn't* any other situation, and it wasn't as simple as that.

Redbone was omitting good, vibrating energy. It was stimulating, and her company was quite enjoyable. I felt her and wanted to get to know her better; I could sense something special about her.

This situation was different; I was sure there was more to this female than a sexual episode. I appreciated the way we maneuvered around each other; it was so comfortable and felt right and natural. It felt familiar. It was a strange and exciting internal debate I was wrestling with myself.

Meanwhile, Redbone was straight cool about everything; she wasn't giving me any indicators she was interested in anything sexual or disseminating any sexual energy. If she did have any desires or fantasies, she concealed them very well. She wasn't misrepresenting herself in any manner. I remained in gentleman mode and continued with our conversation.

HISTORICALLY BLACK LOVE
The Golden Era

We conversed without skipping a beat. No stimulants such as weed or alcohol to propel the tête-à-tête were necessary. There was never an awkward or stagnant moment; everything flowed long and robustly like the Mississippi River. We were so comfortable and relaxed with each other's company that, somehow, I ended up massaging Redbone's shoulders. Her muscles were tight and tense.

The situation to smash couldn't have been any more perfect. The playa in me kept wanting to creep out. I could visualize the whole scenario in the theater of my mind, me softly massaging Redbone's shoulders and slowly sliding my hands down across her plump, firm breast, gently nibbling on her earlobe and softly sucking on her neck. I could visualize myself caressing her inner thighs, getting her warm and moist. The temptation not to give into my lustful desires was the most pressure I had ever experienced. It was as if her D-sized breast were begging and screaming at me to touch them.

The opportunity was there for the taking, an easy layup; still, I resisted and didn't give in by utilizing the most strength I ever had to muster. I pulled from the deepest reservoirs of my soul not to cross the line and give into my temptations.

It felt like I was hanging by my index and middle fingers off a cliff in the Grand Canyon. With every ounce of energy and strength I could command, I fought not to surrender, give in, and let go.

I intuitively understood I had to be strong at this moment. I felt everything, my education, future, and the relationship with this young lady I was feeling, all dangled in the balance and were riding on the consequences of my actions. I had to make the right choice; I couldn't submit to my lustful enticements.

Somehow, someway I found the forte to resist. It was one of the most challenging efforts in my existence not to surrender to my lustful tendencies. I couldn't understand how I got myself into this difficult situation.

I desired Redbone badly but also recognized the timing wasn't right. I also was conscious if I crossed that line, it would be to the point of no return; the burden was massive.

I realized this situation was like no other at that single moment. I had to be feeling something extraordinary for this young lady for me not to put the moves on her. There was a royal quality I recognized and respected. She wasn't, to me at least, a random chic I should smash and dash on. She had something different and felt like a quality investment, and I should take my time to understand what it was.

Our connection was on a level I never had with any female. It was like interlocking Legos; we fit perfectly together; I could feel her differently beyond my six senses.

Suddenly, like osmosis, the notion that she could be the "*One*" popped into my head. A crystal-clear vision of Redbone and I was etched into my mind in a quick flash. I could see myself dressed in an all-white tailored tuxedo equipped with a bow tie and cummerbund. I looked dashingly handsome, sure, and confident with my fresh Caesar haircut with a moon part and a small diamond stud in my left ear.

Redbone is stunningly beautiful. She is draped in an all-white wedding gown that accentuates her shoulders and adorns her figure. Two long curly locks hung from the sides of her lovely face; the rest of her hair was pulled up and neatly tucked under a delicate golden crown. Her earlobes sparkle and reflect the sun with diamond studs. A pearl necklace was hanging around her neck. She is holding a bouquet of white roses. Pink monarch butterflies and hummingbirds fluttered around us as we strolled through a rich green meadow. We were newlyweds. Redbone was pregnant with my first child. We were lost in love.

Then I snapped back into reality. I never envisioned myself with any female in that manner in my young life. I wasn't thinking about settling down with any girl then, and I never considered any female a serious wife or baby mother candidate.

I shook these powerful insights from my mind, glanced at the alarm clock on the dresser, and noticed its digital red numbers screamed 12:07. I was caught off guard and a little disturbed that it was so late. I usually have a good sense of time, but not in this situation. Time seemed to fly in her presence.

I was convinced the longer I lingered in Redbone's space, the more pressure to give in to my temptations would increase. The playa's creed or philosophy was panties dropped after 12; I knew I should leave.

HISTORICALLY BLACK LOVE
The Golden Era

One thing for sure about Redbone, she earned my respect with her grace, intellect, and conversation. Trying to sound mature and responsible, I mentioned that I had to get up early for my work-study, J-O-B.

I caught her off-guard when I prepared to break out; I sensed she was a bit frazzled that I was abruptly bouncing.

As we made our way to the door, the mirror on her desk caught our reflection. We paused for a second as though we were posing for a professional portrait or selfie.

I placed my head next to hers and hugged her waist. She softly stroked my forearm and gently dug her nails into my skin as she squinted her eyes and smirked. Our reflection brought smiles to our faces, acknowledging that we were an attractive young couple.

I followed Redbone to the exit door, down the flowery-smelling hallway trying to conceptualize how I would conclude this evening. I wanted to leave her with a good impression of me. I was feeling Redbone and wanted to spend more time with her, but I didn't know if the feelings were mutual. I wasn't quite sure what to say or do, so I let things continue to flow.

I marveled at how calm, tranquil, and relaxed their apartment was, considering it was a Friday night. I could only imagine the chaos going down on my side of the complex.

HISTORICALLY BLACK LOVE
The Golden Era

When we reached the exit of her suite and walked out onto the balcony, Redbone turned to me. I looked her in the eyes and said,

"I had a delightful time lounging with you; I look forward to the next time we connect."

"I had a delightful time too," she concurred.

"I'll be around all weekend; don't be a stranger."

I wasn't sure how to conclude this evening with Redbone. Should I shake her hand, hug her, or peck her on the cheek? I couldn't determine if she was feeling me or not. She played her cards close to her chest.

I played it safe and extended my right hand. She must have been contemplating the same options but went for the hug. It was awkward—my handshake, her hug, our uncoordinated gestures evolved into our first kiss.

20 First Kiss

I never intended to lock lips with Redbone or experience anything like our first kiss. It was organic and natural; it happened like it was meant to be. The kiss consisted of fairytale magic with all the sparks and fireworks. It was a fantastic, mind-blowing experience on that cool and breezy summer evening.

Redbone stretched up on her tippy toes and draped her arms around my broad shoulders. I gently positioned my hands under her t-shirt and softly caressed the small of her back, feeling the waistband of her panties and the curvature of her plump booty. A soft peck and the tender taste of her tongue did it for me.

The first kiss was an ill experience. I prided myself on avoiding kissing, if possible, as it was too intimate and personal, but Redbone flipped the script. Her intimacy and lips were welcomed and quite alluring.

I desired to experience her body closer to mine and gently tugged her closer so she could feel my strength and physique. I could sense her body temperature rise, erect nipples, and firm breasts pressed against my chest.

Redbone's lips were delicate; the taste buds on her tongue were the texture of a strawberry and tasted like sweet cherry bubble gum.

HISTORICALLY BLACK LOVE
The Golden Era

In real-time, the kiss might have lasted 30 seconds or so. In my mind, it was timelessly infinite. I could have traveled to the furthest edges of the universe and back and not know it.

Yes, the kiss felt like *that*. It was tender, natural, mind-blowing, and couldn't have been any better. It was perfect, our first kiss.

21 Transformation

It was one of the most authentic experiences of my life. It was as though a secret genetic code was activated by the touch of her lips and the sweet taste of her tongue.

A supernatural, biological, and psychological phenomenon occurred from our first kiss. Energy pulsated from the top of my head, down my spine, and throughout my entire body. All my six senses were active and heightened; everything seemed to be magnified by ten.

The conversion was instant. It was as if a bolt of lightning struck me. *BAM!* Just like that, everything changed. I felt more alive than ever. This instant transformation within me strangely felt good and had a certain quality. For the first time, amongst all the other interactions I had with other females, I was absolutely sure about how I felt about Redbone. She was the complete, thoroughly equipped package from a mind, body, and soul perspective. I could seriously rock with her.

Redbone affected me with how a calibrated compass automatically pulls toward a northern direction. With her presence, she gave me purpose and direction. I was confident I would advance and graduate with this female by my side.

My trajectory at Morgan wasn't looking too promising up to that point. I probably would have made it into the spring semester before

I would have to drop out or withdraw from school; things were getting worse for me.

At that moment, I became laser-focused on what I needed to do to keep this female in my life. Our first kiss inspired me to find a way to remain enrolled at Morgan and be with her. She gave me a keener sense of purpose, self, and direction. I grew from a boy to a man; I could feel it all then.

22 The Moment

We both seemed astonished and surprised by how we felt from our first kiss. Like how a circuit breaker explodes with all the sparks, crackling, and popping, accompanied by the smell of burnt electricity and black smoke lingering in the atmosphere while feeling disorientated, that's how I would describe our first kiss. It was a genuinely bugged-out experience.

I struggled to conceal some of what I was now feeling, but I'm sure she saw it on my face *because* I saw it on hers, that stunning amazed look, "Like what just happened?" I didn't plan to kiss her and feel what I felt; it transpired organically.

We both struggled to say goodnight for several minutes. When she finally shut the door to her suite, I stood there on the balcony, perplexed and somewhat confused. I felt strange and completely different. There was something different about me from top to bottom, but I wasn't sure what it could be.

I slowly and cautiously made my way down the three flights of stairs, trying to process the entire evening and these new feelings I was now harboring.

Everything seemed strange and different; the sky, stars, clouds, trees, apartment buildings, and people all seemed to have a yellowish, purplish neon glow or aura around them, even at night. I thought I was bugging out and tried massaging my eyeballs, hoping it would help correct my vision issues.

I was floating on a natural high fueled by Redbone's intoxicating energy. I felt extraordinarily connected to this female that I had just met.

I was missing Redbone already; it was only five minutes since I had left her and five hours since I introduced myself. I desperately wanted to return upstairs and bask in her company and absorb more of her exotic energy. She stimulated me in a novel and different way; I was genuinely intrigued by her in every way.

I never missed any females. One would leave, and I would always have another one coming. Slightly confused about what had just happened, I looked back upstairs from where I had just come from and speculated on the experience I had just shared with Redbone. I wasn't quite sure what had happened, but I knew something serious had just occurred.

Walking back to my suite amongst all the Friday night shenanigans, I began to analyze and ponder the day's events, trying to gain clarity and make sense of the situation.

I reflected on the first time I laid eyes on her, standing in the food line in the refractory, and wondered who this girl was. Our initial and stimulating conversation, the entire lounging session in her suite, the temptations I resisted, the unexpected kiss that blew me away, and these new and eccentric emotions I was now harboring—

all these facts swirled around in my mind while I was trying to process them.

I probed diligently on the last four hours we shared, trying to put things into context with this female I had just met from the Midwest.

Something about her exceptional voice lingered with me; it rang like a New Edition song in my head. Reliving the kiss that gave me life and how it made me feel was so outlandish. How and why was I feeling these strange, foreign, and new feelings? What happened? I was seriously muddled.

I struggled to understand it all; my mind was baffled and blown. I understood something significant was happening to me, and I needed to pay close attention. It was bizarre and new and the oddest feeling or sentiment I had ever experienced.

I then began to speculate what I was feeling or going through seriously. Only one thing kept coming into my mind. No, ... I quickly dismissed the initial notion of what these new feelings could be. Again, after carefully analyzing the entire day and these strange emotions I was now feeling, they returned me to the initial notion.

Nah... but I wasn't sure; I had never felt this way before about any female. Something here is seriously different, and it can't be. Then the idea returned. No, can't it be what I'm feeling? If not, then what could these new feelings be?

HISTORICALLY BLACK LOVE
The Golden Era

After grappling with this new extension of me and what it could be for a fleeting time. BAM! It suddenly made sense; I understood what it was and what I was experiencing. The reality hit me like a ton of bricks.

"Oh shit!"

My 6'2 frame collapsed to its knees on the cobblestone pathway. I clutched my chest as if my heart had been stolen right out of it. I panicked for a second out of shock and utter disbelief when the epiphany of my reality crystallized.

"Oh shit!"

I softly whimpered again, as if I unwillingly submitted to some unidentifiable commanding force I couldn't refute or deny. I was venturing down a pathway I had never traveled with any girl. This was it, the moment, and Redbone was the "One,"

"Oh shit!"

I was transformed into a whole new time and space. I tried to deny with all my strength not to surrender or give in to these new emotions, but my efforts were fruitless. I attempted to deny what I was experiencing in my body, mind, and soul, but I was unsuccessful. I couldn't conceal my spirits or lie to myself. My feelings for Redbone were real and frightening to my core.

HISTORICALLY BLACK LOVE
The Golden Era

"Oh, shit!"

I was caught in a drive-by. Cupid, the Gangsta of Love, had just taken me out.

"Oh shit!

23 A New Awareness

These novel and foreign feelings were intense and tethered to a new sense of awareness. I was experiencing an entirely new self-conscientiousness; my understanding of self-seemed to have expanded with that moment.

A profound sense of freedom, responsibility, and immense vulnerability encapsulated and hit me simultaneously. With this new awareness, I felt my heart thump for the first time; it was an ill experience. I wondered if I was up to the task. Could I manage the pressure and responsibility of this new dynamic in my life? The adjustments are going to be extreme. Just the fact that everything transformed instantly was a lot to process and manage at that time in my young life. It was as if all the females on campus instantly vanished, and Redbone was the only girl my eyes could see.

I understood being in a committed relationship while in college would be a heavy task. Still, I had no choice, Redbone was my destiny, and I knew it.

I was utterly mystified. These new feelings of freedom were so overwhelming that I never knew I could feel this way about a female. Dark, rainy thunderclouds had finally opened, and the bright sunshine was beaming down on me. I was in a great space.

HISTORICALLY BLACK LOVE
The Golden Era

In those few hours that Redbone and I shared, I could completely express and articulate my feelings and thoughts on a whole new stratification. It was easy and comfortable to communicate without pressure. In that brief period, she brought out the best in me. She understood my perspective strangely and uniquely, which emancipated my spirits.

The authentic me was present with this young lady; our undeniable chemistry worked. I felt grounded and at home. I didn't have to make a big production and act like something I wasn't. I didn't need to prove anything to Redbone; I could relax fully in her presence. It was a wonderful place to be, Redbone and me.

This new sense of responsibility was strange and instinctual; a unique maturity within me had awakened. I felt, for the first time, a sense of certainty. I *knew* for sure how I felt. I couldn't visualize going part-time with Redbone; it was all or nothing. A commitment was necessary to make this situation blossom to its fullest potential.

I never rationalized wanting and needing to be with any female in a relationship; now, I was willing to do whatever was required to get and maintain Redbone in my orbit.

The emotions of being vulnerable were real and quite alarming too. For the first time, I realized my feelings were real and exposed. What was even scarier is I now understood my heart could be broken; Redbone would be the only one who would be equipped to do it.

HISTORICALLY BLACK LOVE
The Golden Era

The insecurity was one of the most uncomfortable positions I ever found myself in, especially on the campus of an HBCU. Too many dogs roamed around campus like me, which was too much pressure.

I wasn't sure how I would manage this new mental state. What if Redbone wasn't feeling anything I was feeling? How will I be able to deal with that scenario? How could she even be feeling *half* of what I was? My mind was all over the place, trying to figure things out.

Before Redbone, I never invested parts of my heart into any situation or relationship, but this was different. I had genuine feelings for the first time.

It was scary to know I could feel so vulnerable that I was shaking. I always thought I would choose the woman I'd fall in love with; I had no choice in this matter; love chose *me*.

I might have been fascinated by a pretty face or even said I loved a couple of females. Still, I swiftly grasped that my feelings for Redbone were more profound and on a whole other level than anything I had ever experienced.

All those other so-called relationships were cosmetic, surface, or physical; this current situation was a whole new ball game, played on a different level. I wanted and *needed* Redbone; she melted my ice-cold heart, which was as simple as that.

HISTORICALLY BLACK LOVE
The Golden Era

I understood how a young lady could enchant a young man for the first time. I often thought love was like a great love song. Its words and melodies invoked unique feelings and emotions when you heard them, but when it was over, so were the sentiments. They just vanished, but this wasn't the case anymore. Instead, my feelings about Redbone were deeply embedded within me; they were akin to a starburst or an organic berth. It was naturally intense.

I was that guy who didn't care if the shorty on my radar had a man or not; I was going to shoot my shot regardless. Now the tables could be turned on me instantly. What if some dude was firing his shot at Redbone? That notion made me sick and almost made me lose my mind. How could I be feeling this way in such a brief time?

Although my feelings were authentic, I wasn't ready for love. I had no real money to finance a relationship. I struggled to find myself and my purpose while trying to navigate through school. I was insecure in many ways and not ready to give my heart to a woman, but I had no choice. I had to push on and apply some faith. I understood I must be strong in the moment of my weakness, manage my business, and lock shorty down.

24 Crying with Coltrane

Although there were still a few stragglers hanging around, it was nothing to the degree before I left. The activity had died down significantly and migrated to another suite after the Finals.

When I arrived back in my room, Fifty Grand was awake and still nursing on the same bottle of Old Granddad he copped earlier. He was lying in his bed, relaxing with his long-ashy legs crossed, enumerated while the sounds of Coltrane's saxophone consumed our cluttered room.

His passion for jazz music was equal to mine for Hip-Hop. His knowledge was extensive; he could put everything about Jazz into a historical context, just as in-depth as I could with Hip-Hop. He tried to give me an education on Jazz music and its rich history at every opportunity afforded to him.

"You know Jazz is considered America's first true Indigenous art form. The rhythmic beats from the drums of enslaved Africans were a form of wireless communication to communicate to other tribe's long distances away. Over centuries the beating of the drums evolved into a musical art form of improvisation, spiritual tranquility, and some aspects of voodoo. New Orleans was the genesis during the late 1800s and evolved into what it is today, a massive force in music and enjoyed by millions all around the globe."

HISTORICALLY BLACK LOVE
The Golden Era

I would flip the script on him and follow up with some Hip-Hop historical facts to balance his persistence that I learn something about Jazz music.

"You know, Hip-Hop's birthplace is the South Bronx. It jumped off in the Soundview Project's recreation center on August 11, 1973. At 1520 Cedrick Ave, DJ Kool Herc, short for Hercules, was DJing his baby sister's, *Going Back to School* party and had set up two turntables, some big ass house speakers, and encouraged the partygoers to say something on the mic while he played certain breakbeats from certain portions of records. From that day on, Hip-Hop has evolved into an expressive art form and has morphed into a worldwide phenomenon, spanning the globe throughout all parts of Europe, Asia, and South America. Hip-Hop is the most consumed and lucrative genre of all the world's music. The Indigenous, urban American music generates thousands of employment opportunities and billions in revenue annually."

Fifty was in love with Coltrane; his compositions would touch his soul to the point they would sometimes bring him to tears. He meditated to Coltrane while engaged in a complicated equation or a project. He'd tried to convince me to listen to more Jazz, saying there were plenty of intellectual benefits to listening to it. I liked and appreciated some jazz, but I was only feeling Hip-Hop at the time.

Now I'm suddenly feeling this Redbone I just met from the Midwest.

Fifty popped up, lowered the volume to the Coltrane CD, and hit me with questions about the night's escapades.

HISTORICALLY BLACK LOVE
The Golden Era

What's good, homie?" he inquired.

"Did you smash? Was she a freak? Did you get any dome? What happened, homie?"

Slumped at my desk and staring up at the ceiling, I attempted to make some sense of what I was currently experiencing. It happened so fast; I was trying to wrap my mind around it. I thought I'd have to invest more time, capital, and energy into a situation in order to be feeling this way.

I reflected on all the other females I was involved with; Redbone was the premium, top-notch, and closest to my perfect as perfect could be, from the inside and out. I reflected on my past, contemplated my current situation, and constructed my future based on this one female. She was the only female I could visualize having my children. Shit was crazy; nothing made sense. One minute I'm a playa for life, and the next, I'm head over heels for this one girl. In some respects, I felt trapped. I had not planned any of this and was not ready to surrender my heart to any female. What was I going to do?

I didn't say a word to Fifty; I just sat there zoning out to the music of Coltrane's "Supreme Love." It was the soundtrack to how I felt then, emotional and scattered all over the place. *"A love supreme, a love supreme, a love supreme, a love supreme, a love supreme...."*

Fifty inquired 10 minutes later.

HISTORICALLY BLACK LOVE
The Golden Era

"Colie, what happened? What is she all about?"

'Yo, - I – think - I'm - in – love – with - Redbone,"

I slowly replied as I was still gazing into outer space in my mind,

"Seriously- B."

"What are you talking about, Coli?"

Fifty held a bewildered and disgusting look on his face. He seemed disappointed in me. I was supposed to be a *playa* and his inspiration. It was like I was letting him down. Fifty sensed the seriousness of the situation by the tone of my voice, body language, and overall demeanor and fell back with the questions.

"Yo, this nigga just met the shorty today and already fell in love." He said aloud.

"You are a sucker for love, Colie, a sucker for love."

In a gesture of disgust, Fifty turned up the volume of Coltrane and took another swig from the bottle.

"Yeah, you are a sucker for love."

25 The Next Day

I didn't get much sleep. I tossed and turned most of the night, thinking about Redbone. The kiss we'd shared hunted me while continuously swirling around in my head. I was confused, trying to make some sense of these strange feelings for and about this female. Everything about Redbone intrigued me—her looks, smell, taste, mind, and energy. I did my best to evade these feelings, but it was useless. I was hit.

Around 6 A.M., while Fifty and everybody in our suite were still passed out, I jumped into the shower and let the steamy hot water run over my face as I tried to cleanse Redbone from my brain. After a long hot, meditating shower, I threw on some sweats and headed to the refractory on a solo mission. I needed time to myself to figure things out and get my mind right.

The sun was about to introduce itself to the morning Baltimore sky. The refractory was populated with a few early birds.

My meal consisted of buttered grits, scrambled cheese eggs, whole wheat, buttered toast with strawberry jam, and a tall glass of ice-cold orange juice.

I isolated myself by sitting way in the back up against the wall in the sparsely populated cafeteria. I gingerly placed some grits and eggs on top of the jammed toast, folded in half, and compressed it with my hands before slowly biting into it. With every morsel of food, I chewed, I relived every moment of the night before, wondering if what I had experienced had happened or if it was all a dream. Then I was bugged that I would even think in such a manner. Finally, after an hour of sitting by myself contemplating the events from last night, I gathered up my scattered thoughts and headed to my work-study job. My equilibrium was off for sure.

I was working for the on-campus Housing Department. My primary responsibilities included cleaning and changing all air filters of the vacant housing units on campus. It was a summer stipend program, and most of the school's football players and other athletes were employed by it. It wasn't demanding, and our boss Mr. J was a cool, older gentleman.

I was building relationships with many football players and was seriously considering going out for the team, a Division 1 AA program. I was apprehensive because they had a losing record for the last decade or more, and I wasn't sure if I wanted to put my ego through such trauma. But playing football would be my last effort to keep me in school if necessary.

While at work, I couldn't do anything. I was so unproductive; all I could do was think of Redbone. I couldn't shake her or the kiss. I found myself gazing out the eighth-floor window of an empty dorm room in Blount Towers most of the afternoon, caught up in the rapture of Redbone, trying to digest it all.

Never in my life had I felt like I did for this one girl. Everything seemed out of character, and I felt off-balance like I was infected by the flu or recovering from a Mike Tyson knockout blow.

HISTORICALLY BLACK LOVE
The Golden Era

After work of basically doing nothing but thinking about this one girl, I made a beeline back to my room. I attempted to read up on *Things Fall Apart* by Chinua Achebe, the reading assignment for the summer English course. I couldn't get past the first page, let alone the first paragraph. Regardless, I couldn't comprehend anything then; Redbone was constantly on my mind.

For the remainder of the weekend, I intentionally avoided Redbone, hoping that my feelings would subside. I rationalized that she couldn't feel half of anything I was experiencing; I did my best to stay out of sight and off the grid.

For the next few days, I would go to the refractory very early in the morning, just when it opened, or late in the evening, just before the facility closed. I stayed away from all social functions, settings, and circles. I didn't want to run into Redbone yet; I was trying to sort out my complicated thoughts and feelings. I realized this was a demanding situation for me; it was life-altering.

I mentally and physically begin preparing myself to manage the tidal wave of emotion and events I anticipated coming my way. I had heard about this situation from older men; the moment a young man fell in love with a woman, it was happening to me.

26 Preparing for Love

Love, it had to be by the way I was now feeling, thinking, and behaving. I was in love with a young lady for the first time. Nothing was expected or experienced before; it was all new to me.

All those wild stories told to me by my drunk uncles and older men I looked up to, which I thought were outlandish exaggerations of how love will make a man feel and act, were true. It was my time and turn; there was nothing that I could do but accept my fate. I was experiencing "The Jones."

At that time, I longed to converse with my father to help guide me through this complicated process. I recalled how he attentively explained the birds and the bees to me.

I was fourteen and experiencing puppy love with Rhonda, a dark skin, thick female from Cleveland, Ohio. She was two years older than me and lived right next door. I still can smell and feel her greasy jury curl juice running down the sides of my face. My father had a keen eye and observed how much time we were spending together and how intimate our relationship was becoming. It was time for the *Talk*.

My Dad sat me on my bed and broke down, sexual intercourse in plain and straightforward terms I could understand. After educating me about the male and female anatomies and how they functioned, the importance of being responsible, and the consequences of not using a condom and respecting the young lady, the most critical aspect of our conversation was something else he said.

"Son, remember this, you don't have to be in love with a woman to have sex with her, but the best and most satisfying and fulfilling sex is when you're in love with the female you're having sex with; it's called making love, which is different than having sexual intercourse. To make love to a woman is a special privilege and shouldn't be taken for granted. She is the woman you want to invest your heart, time, and energy into and consider marrying and constructing your life around."

Later that spring, I was locked out of my house; my father and brothers went to pick my mother up from the Louisville Airport to attend Shawn's, my oldest brother's Fort Knox High School graduation. Next door, I discovered Rhonda was home alone; her mother was away for the weekend. We cuddled up on the couch, watching Video Soul with Donny Simpson and Sherri Carter, ordered a pepperoni pizza from Munchie's, and lost our virginity while Whitney Houston's, *Saving All My Love for You* softly played in the background. It was a quick minute or so if that. We did use a Jimmy Hat, as my father instructed. I could have used his wisdom and insight on my matter of love.

At that time, I didn't have anyone I fully trusted to assist me in sorting out what I was feeling and help me navigate this significant aspect of my life. I was in love, alone, and far away from home. I did have Fifty Grand, but he wasn't well-versed in the opposite sex. He was a nerd. I had to figure this out on my own and jump out the window.

HISTORICALLY BLACK LOVE
The Golden Era

Since the Friday night mind-blowing kiss, I was ultra-focused and inspired to do whatever was necessary to remain enrolled at Morgan and keep Redbone by my side. The plan was to get a jump start on the registration and loan process complexities. I was all about business now; it was no time for procrastinating.

Early Tuesday morning, I checked in with my Supervisor, Mr. Johnson, who we all called "*Mr. J*"—a large, lofty, seasoned dark-skinned man. He was a no-bullshit, straight-up-and-down kind of guy. If you kept it real with him, Mr. J was one hundred with you.

I carefully articulated to Mr. J that I wanted and needed to prepare for the Fall semester with the registration, financial-aid aspects, and the whatnot. I bargained that if he could give me the morning off, I'd work it off later.

Mr. J was cool with my proposal and permitted me to handle my business. I sincerely thanked him, grabbed a raisin bran muffin and a big red apple from the refectory, then jumped onto the campus shuttle to be transported to the Financial Aid offices in Northwood.

To my surprise, the office was packed with students trying to get registered early. The process was enduring; you had to stand in these long snail-moving lines, fill out mountains of paperwork, apply for FAFSA loans and Pell grants, inquire about scholarships, and tolerate some unprofessional, short-tempered staff trying to get the correct information filed.

It took the entire morning to get the ball rolling on this paperwork. Back then, during the Golden Era, we didn't have cell phones or

HISTORICALLY BLACK LOVE
The Golden Era

social media with YouTube, Facebook, and Twitter to occupy our minds while we stood in long lines; you just had to have endurance and patients.

As I walked out of the financial aid offices of Northwood for the first time at Morgan, I felt like a student with a purpose. I seriously considered what I wanted to study and build a successful career around.

It was a beautiful afternoon; the sun hung high and bright at the top of the clear blue afternoon sky. I managed well at avoiding Redbone and hadn't seen her since our mind-blowing interaction Friday evening. She was heavy on my mind all the time, every second of the day, in a good way. The essence of her touch, smell, and kiss made me feel so good and vibrant; her energy was perfect. I couldn't wait to see her again.

After completing all the necessary paperwork that afternoon, I needed to head back to campus for my 1:30 English Literature class. It was in Holmes Hall, way on the other side of the campus. Instead of catching the shuttle, I had a solid hunch to walk to class for some strange reason. It also was an intentional effort to avoid Redbone and all others. I wasn't ready to interact with anyone until I got my thoughts and mind right.

I *never* walked. I would always catch the shuttle onto the main campus, get off at the McKeldin Center, order some chicken wings from the canteen, socialize a bit, and then bounce to class. However, I was in my loner mode this afternoon, and strolling up Hillen Road was the less-traveled route, or so I thought. I attempted to develop a strategy to get this young lady into my life.

As I crossed Hillen Road and ventured up the street, I daydreamed about this female I had just met and only chilled with once. At that moment, I realized I didn't know exactly how to pronounce her name. I knew it had something to do with the number three, but my dyslexic mind couldn't retrieve her name then. Even though I didn't know her name, she had been in my head since we met every second of the day.

Thousands of high-def mini-movie scenarios played in my mind on repeat about Redbone and the next time we bumped into one another. I asked myself hundreds of thought-provoking questions like, what were my intentions with this young lady? What if she has a special friend? What if she wasn't feeling me or anything I was feeling? What if she is a *playa* and has several dudes on the side? Could I handle the pressure of having one girl on campus? What if another nigga tried to shoot his shot at Redbone? Could I be committed to her? What will I convey to her the next time we encounter one another? Could she be my bride and the mother of my seeds? That kiss was so fabulous.

My thoughts kept cycling back to the frightening notion: what if she wasn't feeling anything close to what I was experiencing? The idea struck terror in my heart because I knew how I felt; I was feeling Redbone and wanted her to be my only girl.

While ironing out the details of my master plan of getting her into my life, I unsuspectedly walked past a Maryland Transportation Authority MTA bus stop. It was the kind of bus stop with an enclosed partition and bench to protect the riders from punitive weather waiting for transit.

As I strolled past the bus stop, I noticed a person sitting and waiting for the bus. I recognize it's a female, but I pay her little to no mind, heavily immersed in the thought of Redbone and the construction of my plan. I quickly glanced at the female sitting as I walked by her. My eyes connected with this female; her lips and face looked familiar.

I did a double-take; I thought my mind was playing tricks on me. Suddenly, like magic, conforming to the exact specifications of the thoughts and images in my head, the female sitting on the bench morphed into Redbone from Friday night; bam, instantly! Just like that, Redbone appeared to be sitting on the bus stop bench.

I was completely mesmerized and blown away. It felt like I was in a scene straight out of *The Matrix*. It was as if a program was uploaded onto my operating system, and instantly Redbone appeared at the bus stop, sucking on a lollipop.

I was bugging, trying to keep my composure, thinking to myself, this can't be real; this can't be Redbone, the girl I have been missing, thinking, and dreaming about for the last few days, even though I wanted it to be her, it was unbelievable that it was her.

The only female to truly blow my mind and occupy every corner of my head for every second of the last seventy-two hours was suddenly in my presence. I thought I was bugging it just seemed so unreal.

I was spooked in the truest sense because of the amount of time I was investing in thinking about her and how I wanted her in my life, and then instantly, she appeared alive and in the flesh. It was heavy and difficult to process at that time fully.

Caught entirely off guard, I became lite headed; my legs turned into wet spaghetti. I had to grab hold of the partition to maintain my balance so I wouldn't topple onto the sidewalk and embarrass myself. It was that serious.

It wasn't in the plan to link up with her until the weekend. Maybe at a party, some social function on campus, or back in the refractory, but *never* in a million years could I have imagined meeting up with her again at a Baltimore City bus stop. The odds seemed astronomical and unfathomable.

In all my time at Morgan, this was the second time in one week that I ran into this girl I had never seen before on campus. I quickly calculated the odds and knew this situation had a divine essence; there is no such thing as a coincidence.

At first, I didn't recognize Redbone; she was dolled entirely up from top to bottom, her hair-doe, gold hoop earrings, bright, colorful Tommy Hilfiger jacket, denim jeans, and Reebok Fifty-Four elevens. Her appearance and vibe were a complete upgrade from Friday night's casual appearance. She projected a sexy aura that was absent Friday night and looked like she was representing Brooklyn.

HISTORICALLY BLACK LOVE
The Golden Era

I was caught off guard and a little confused by how attractive she was for a second. Initially, I wasn't sure this was the same female from Friday night; she shined bright like a diamond.

She must have recognized me instantly by the way she literally pounced into my arms with an unconscious, animalistic attraction or reflex. Redbone quickly regained her composure, but I peeped at her instinctual response towards me and my presence. She was feeling and missing me too. I was comforted to have that little golden nugget of insight; I could relax a little more.

Completely caught off guard and nervous. At the same time, I was calm, ultra focused, and relaxed. All my planning and preparation were irrelevant at this point; it was either do or die. I embraced the moment and swung for the bleachers. I concentrated entirely on her, getting into my zone.

I wasn't dressed to impress; I wore a T-shirt and basketball shorts. I could've used a fresh haircut or a tight lineup. By the sparkle in Redbone's eyes, my appearance didn't matter. I could see she was pleased to see me again.

Redbone was on the cusp of womanhood, that delicate and precious time when a young lady began to bloom into a woman, such a breathtaking sight. Her hair had a soft sheen into these big, bouncy curls that drooped down to her shoulders.

HISTORICALLY BLACK LOVE
The Golden Era

Her youthful beauty, clear lip balm, and golden caramel complexion shimmered intensely under the Baltimore sun. I stood there for a few seconds and soaked her beauty up. Every time I see her, it gets better and better. She was baby doll pretty.

27 Reunion

"I have been looking for you these last couple of days?" "It's like you vanished off campus. I don't have time to play games, where have you been?

Demanded Redbone in a slightly agitated but convivial tone. Her hands were on her hips, slightly rotating her neck as she sternly pointed her index finger in my face, looking so fine as she wanted to be while bitching at me. I could sense she was happy to see me again. Redbone was checking me as though I was her man like we were already in a committed relationship.

I was attempting to play it off like she wasn't occupying substantial portions of my mind while simultaneously trying to remain relaxed and sounding somewhat responsible and mature. I cleared my throat and carefully crafted a response.

"I apologize. I have been managing my business, you know, getting things situated for the Fall semester. Financial aid, scholarships, room and board, meal plan, my schedule, and the whole nine yards. I want to ensure there are no problems when the Fall rolls around."

"Yeah, I understand; those are important priorities," she replied.

HISTORICALLY BLACK LOVE
The Golden Era

"Wow, you look amazing. I almost didn't recognize it was you. Your whole style is completely transformed from Friday nights; I'm feeling those Shirley Temple curls; they look great on you; you wear them well."

She smiled, "Yes, it's one of my many superpowers; I can transform like that; I use them from time to time."

"Ok, Superwoman, I see you, I see you."

Redbone mentioned she was in route to the other shopping plaza a few miles up Perring Parkway. She needed to retrieve a few things from the store to help her get situated with the summer semester. She also intended to return the curling iron she was holding in a gray plastic bag. Her hair was all dolled up; I'm sure she used the curling iron to hook up her hair.

"How are you doing? What have you been up to?" I'd inquired.

"I'm managing, still knee-deep in studying for the state education exam. I'll be so relieved when it's all over. I thought my friend would stop by this weekend and help me study. I even cooked dinner, but my friend was a no-show."

While grilling me with a face, saying where were you, and why didn't you stop by?

"What did you cook?" I asked.

HISTORICALLY BLACK LOVE
The Golden Era

"Veal with Swiss cheese, broccoli, and buttered pasta. I ate dinner myself".

"Sounds like a tasty, healthy meal."

"How would you know; you didn't stop by to see about me. But you were 'managing your business,' right?"

The sarcasm was evident on her face and in her mid-west accent.

"You sound as though you have been missing a brother?" I cracked a smile.

"Maybe I was, but you wouldn't know unless you stopped by!"

Staring directly into her corneas, she was utterly present; there was no deceit or deception in her eyes; she was ready, for sure and had her mind made up. She knew what she wanted, and so did I.

Redbone continued to insinuate and emphasize how sourly disappointed she was that she didn't see me over the weekend. She wiped a thin curl that dangled across her pretty face to the side— fluctuating her voice with some attitude and rotating her neck to stress her point that I needed to stop by.

HISTORICALLY BLACK LOVE
The Golden Era

"You know I stay in the same apartment complex as you, on the opposite side, on the third floor? The same apartment you'd visited on Friday?"

She asked matter-of-factly, illustrating her point by putting her three fingers about an inch from my face.

"You didn't forget where I am staying? It's apartment 327."

Suddenly, a late-modeled Baltimore City bus aggressively screeches up to the bus stop in the next moment. The worn mechanical doors forcefully collapsed open. The bus driver is a chubby white man with rosy cheeks and is wearing an impatient look on his face. His demeanor gave the impression that he was running late and didn't have a second to spare while we conversed. Redbone and I were receptive to his vibe.

She sternly pointed her finger in my face and demanded I visit her later.

"Stop by tonight, around seven-dish."

At that moment, everything became surreal. I felt discombobulated while time seemed to slow down while reality continuously swirled in motion around us. It felt like we were the only ones on Earth. I sensed the dynamics shifting, I'm aware something is about to transpire, but I'm oblivious to what it could be.

HISTORICALLY BLACK LOVE
The Golden Era

Redbone approached me, effortlessly penetrating my force field of personal space, elevated up on her tippy toes, glanced directly into my soul, softly palmed my cheeks with her soft hands, and placed the juiciest tenderest loveliest kiss my lips have ever felt.

It was undeniable, the truest, and so satisfying. I felt love on her lips; my whole head was blown by how she took the liberty and had the assurance to kiss me. I was surprised by her sweet gesture of affection; it was wholly unexpected but quite welcoming, like Friday night's kiss.

I heard Redbone softly exhale as she looked deep into my eyes after the kiss. At that moment, I was utterly content and convinced she was special.

I could now relax a little more; my feelings were not in vain. Redbone was feeling, wanting, and missing me too. The additional kiss solidified our connection and confirmed she was the "One," it was without a doubt.

She again demanded I stop through.

"I'll see you tonight around seven." She emphatically stated as she flashed her pearly white smile and turned to board the transit.

As I watched this pretty young thing pay her fare, I marveled at how beautiful and sexy she was and how good she made me feel. I felt fully alive, vibrating like I could accomplish anything.

HISTORICALLY BLACK LOVE
The Golden Era

Our eyes connected through the smudged-up bus windows as it gaggled up Hillen Road and faded out of sight.

I stood there stunned and amazed, thinking about what had just emerged. The entire situation seemed like a storybook dream that manifested right before my eyes. It was unbelievable, and a higher power certainly had a hand in this exceptional circumstance.

What I experienced this past week was close to impossible; everything fell into place perfectly. The work-study opportunity, the room and board, a stipend, and, to top everything off with a cherry, Redbone, a girl I was feeling and wanted, was feeling and wanting me too.

When I was running out of options, on the verge of everything collapsing, and me having to drop out of school, my universe and outlook all changed in the most remarkable of ways. My education, relationships, and love all meant something new to me. I knew I discovered why I wanted and needed to be at Morgan; everything felt proper and exact with Redbone now in the picture. It was a gift from above; it had to be. How else could I explain things? I simply couldn't and accepted it as a blessing.

I also pondered Friday night. I was grateful I had the strength not to surrender and give in to my lustful temptations. I understood how vital that moment was. I'm sure I would have dismantled something divine and unique. I felt like I matured substantially in such a way I was greatly rewarded; our relationship was now worth ten folds, without a doubt.

HISTORICALLY BLACK LOVE
The Golden Era

I also understood that the sky was the limit with this Redbone by my side. I knew that I would earn my degree and graduate for sure. Amazed without any doubt, my dream girl was a reality.

As I continued to make my way up Hillen Road, walking on cloud nine to class, I gently massaged the remnants of Redbone's lip balm onto my lips, trying to preserve her lovely essence with me for as long as possible.

Then it hit me, damn. I forgot to get Redbones' name.

Thank You

I graduated in '97 with a Bachelor's in Science in Media Communications with Second Honors. My peers, colleagues, and professors also recognized me with the Most Outstanding Television Student Award for the class of ninety-seven. President Bill Clinton delivered the commencement speech at my graduation.

Thank you, Redbone, for coming into my life just in time. You loved me when I needed it the most. You were my first and only true love, my Superwoman. I couldn't have accomplished any of this without you. I love you.

Sincerely,

Danny M. Coles

Made in the USA
Middletown, DE
08 September 2023

37769617R00116